'No! Don't go into the fog! You'll never j...

When Rachel's parents get jobs on an offshore island, her main worry is when the wind turbine will be installed so that she can play her CDs. But then she notices some weird things happening. Her brother, Stevie, always untidy, insists that everything in his room should be in straight lines, facing the same way. The island rabbits dig their burrows in parallel lines, facing north. Why don't the Islanders get lost in the fog? And why did the last warden's house burn down? As she tries to find the answers to these mysteries, Rachel has to act quickly to prevent another tragedy.

SUSAN GATES was born in Grimsby in 1950. She has a degree in English and American Literature from Warwick University and a Dip.Ed. from Coventry College of Education. She has taught in secondary schools in Africa and for eight years in a comprehensive school in County Durham. She has also taught in a technical college and on YTS and Community Task Force Schemes. She is married and has three children.

Also by Susan Gates

African Dreams
ISBN 0 19 271684 0

'Susan Gates has an impressive understanding of the feelings which drive young people . . . reading *African Dreams* will be a valuable social education as well as a pleasure.'
The School Librarian

Raider
ISBN 0 19 271644 1
Commended for the Carnegie Medal

'. . . it is still possible to find new fiction that can be read even next year, or later, or twice by the same reader. *Raider* is one for a start.'
The Observer

Firebug
ISBN 0 19 271735 9

When Callum sets fire to his own home, he sets off a terrifying chain of events which could trigger a major ecological disaster. Through it all, the squirrel seems to be the only thing Callum can rely on.

Iron Heads

Other books by Susan Gates

The Burnhope Wheel
The Lock
Dragline
Deadline for Danny's Beach
African Dreams
Raider
Firebug

Iron Heads

Susan Gates

Oxford University Press

Oxford New York Toronto

Oxford University Press, Great Clarendon Street, Oxford OX2 6DP

Oxford New York
Athens Auckland Bangkok Bogota Bombay
Buenos Aires Calcutta Cape Town Dar es Salaam Delhi
Florence Hong Kong Istanbul Karachi
Kuala Lumpur Madras Madrid Melbourne
Mexico City Nairobi Paris Singapore
Taipei Tokyo Toronto

and associated companies in
Berlin Ibadan

Oxford is a trade mark of Oxford University Press
Copyright © Susan Gates 1997
First published 1997

A CIP catalogue record for this book is available
from the British Library

Cover illustration by Paul Wright
ISBN 0 19 271755 3

Printed and bound in Great Britain by
Biddles Ltd, Guildford and King's Lynn

1

'No! Don't go into the fog! You'll never find your way out!'

But the three little kids I'm yelling at are down on the beach, too far away to hear me.

I can't believe it. They watched the fog, same as me. Stood and watched while it poured out of the sand dunes, like it does every morning on Pilot Island.

Anyone with brains would've got out of its way, fast. But they're just standing there, letting it roll closer and closer.

They've lived all their lives on Pilot Island. They must know about the fog. I've only just moved here with my mum and dad and my brother Stevie. But even I know about it.

'Wait until the morning fog clears,' my dad warned me and Stevie. 'Don't go down to the beach while it's still there. It's really dangerous. You could get lost in it. Never find your way back home. You could be walking out to sea and never realize it!'

He especially warned my brother because Stevie has got no sense of direction. Even though he's eleven he can't tell right from left. He can't put his shoes on the right feet, or tie the shoe-laces. He puts his clothes on back to front and inside out. He gets himself into real muddles. But the psychologist said that's not his fault. It's not because he's stupid or lazy or anything. It's because of what's wrong with him.

But those kids I'm watching, they must *really* be stupid. Didn't their mums and dads warn them about the fog?

Everyone knows that Pilot Island is foggy a lot of the time. My dad went on and on about it until we were really scared. But those island kids aren't a bit scared. They're just laughing at the fog. Dancing about in front of it, like they're daring it to get them. Like they're playing some kind of game.

But if they're not worried why should I be? And anyhow, why should I try to warn them—those island kids aren't exactly friendly.

So I tell myself, 'Mind your own business, Rachel,' and close my bedroom window again.

But I keep on spying at the island kids from behind my curtains. I don't know why.

When they laugh they open their blue lips wide and their mouths look like blue caves. I can't get used to those bright blue mouths, even though I've been on this island for a whole month. They still give me the creeps.

It's because they chew skyberries all the time. Skyberries grow on bushes in the sand dunes. They're bright blue with orange seeds inside. My dad's thrilled about them. He's practically hopping about with excitement. He says things like, 'Skyberries are fascinating flora. They're packed full of minerals. And they're unique to Pilot Island. You don't find them anywhere else in the world!'

Me and Stevie just yawn, 'Yeah, great, Dad, great.' But Pilot Island is a nature reserve and my dad's just landed a job as warden. So he's bound to get excited about the plants and the wildlife and stuff like that.

I'm still doing some sneaky spying at those island kids. They're going 'ha, ha, ha' at the fog with their blue skyberry mouths. All the kids on Pilot Island are skyberry crazy. They pick them straight off the bushes. They eat them dried as well, like little blue raisins. They always have some stashed in their pockets. They even wear them round their necks, like necklaces of bright blue beads. They nibble them when they feel like a snack.

My mum said, 'Skyberries are like sweets to these island children.'

That's pitiful, isn't it? These poor island kids can't buy Snickers or Mars Bars or Crunchies. Because there are no shops on Pilot Island. Not a single one. It's like living in prehistoric times.

There are no cars, except for the warden's jeep. There's no electricity even. Dad said, 'Don't worry, Rach. We'll have our own personal wind turbine right next to the house. We'll make our own electricity.'

But our wind turbine wasn't here when we moved in. It got held up. It's coming next week though. Good. I'm sick of using smelly old oil lamps and having to heat up water to wash my hair.

Would you believe it, the people on Pilot Island don't want electricity? So the poor island kids can never watch telly or play on computers. That's child cruelty if you ask me. And they can't go to the pictures or bowling or to McDonald's. The island people don't like going off the island. They don't believe in it. They think: Life on Pilot Island—GOOD; life on the mainland—BAD. They even say going to the mainland makes them sick. I said to Mum, 'That's just stupid!'

But Mum got mad with me. She said, '*Shhhhh! Shhhhh!* Don't let anyone hear you say that. We're incomers here. We're mainlanders. We've got to respect their way of life.'

Respect, my bottom! If I think something's stupid I'll say so.

What's going on down on the beach? Better check up. My breath has misted the window and I can't see out so I have to rub a little spy-hole. Those three island kids are

3

still messing about down there. The fog's creeping closer, closer. Soon it'll swallow them up. But they couldn't care less.

Suddenly a chill goes right through me. The shock of it makes me grab the curtains, screw them up tight in my fist.

'Stevie!'

My brother's out there. I take another good look through the spy-hole. No mistake. It's Stevie all right.

He's laughing a blue laugh, just like the other two. I don't know why but that makes the hairs tingle on the back of my neck.

I should have spotted Stevie before because he doesn't look like an island kid. They all look the same — skinny with floppy black hair and green eyes and snooty long noses. (They're inbred, my dad said.) And Stevie is sort of chunky with spiky brown hair. But it was the blue laugh that fooled me. I thought Stevie was one of them. I knew he'd been hanging around with some island children. But I didn't know he'd started eating skyberries.

I open the window and yell. 'Stevie, get back here now! What do you think you're doing?'

Stevie's Special Needs at school. He doesn't *look* like there's anything wrong with him, but he gets lost in supermarkets. He can't run either — his feet get tangled and trip him up. So if Stevie got lost in the fog and the tide came in he wouldn't stand a chance.

He can't hear me. Or he's pretending not to. He's stubborn my brother. He likes to pretend he doesn't need help.

This morning I said, 'You'll fall over those shoe-laces. Come here. I'll tie them for you.'

He got really mad. His face went all red and he yelled. 'No way! I like them dangling like this. It's cool!'

4

But it's got nothing to do with being cool. It's because he can't tie them himself. Even though he's eleven years old.

I don't want to go out there. Not while those island kids are around. They've got this weird way of looking at you . . . They've got eyes like clear green seawater.

Suppose I have to go out there though. In case Stevie needs looking after. But that's nothing new. I've been looking after Stevie for almost all of my life.

I sigh, 'Here we go again, Rach,' as I pull on my jeans.

I'm not rushing. It's not all that urgent this time. Not like the time he got stuck in the revolving doors. Or the time he nearly strangled himself with his backpack. I don't think Stevie will go into the fog. He may be Special Needs, but that doesn't mean he's stupid.

When I walk past Stevie's bedroom the door is open.

It's like World War Three happened in there. There are clothes and books and junk all over the place.

The psychologist told Mum that kids like Stevie can't organize themselves—it's not his fault if he's a total mess. So Mum never shouts at him about it. Sometimes he trashes his room deliberately. And Mum doesn't shout at him, even then. You know why? Because it's bad for his self-esteem. The psychologist said so.

Self-esteem, my bottom! I get nearly killed if my bedroom's a tip.

As I pass the kitchen window I take a quick peek out, just to check the situation.

'Oh, no.'

I've changed my mind. It's urgent.

The fog's moving faster than I thought. Much faster. It's swelling, into a giant blob monster. It's got squirmy arms, reaching out for Stevie and the island kids.

'Run, Stevie, run!'

I'm out of the back door now, sliding down dunes, crashing through skyberry bushes.

The berries get squelched as I smash my way through.

I'm yelling my head off: 'Stevie, keep out of the fog!'

Beyond the fog is the sea. The tide's coming in. You can hear it rumbling, like pebbles rolling round in a giant cement mixer.

'Stevie!'

I'm worried now. Running like my heart'll burst.

It's too late. I'm on top of a dune gasping for breath when it happens. They're right below me, all three of them. Like in a slow-motion film they stand there, laughing bright blue laughs. And then slowly, slowly, they let the fog roll right over them, like a river of white smoke.

It closes over their heads. For a second I see three grey ghosts in the fog. And then—nothing at all.

'Stevie, can you hear me?'

I turn around. Our brand-new house isn't there any more. Everything feels really hushed and still. I go scrambling to the bottom of the dune.

'Stevie!'

Some wispy bits of fog come floating up round me.

Then, gulp, it's got me. Swallowed me up. It's swallowing the whole of Pilot Island, from end to end.

'Where are you, Stevie?'

He could be somewhere very close. I could stretch out my hand, maybe grab him.

'Stevie?'

He doesn't answer. All I grab is a fistful of fog. There's just silence—like all the clocks in the world have stopped.

What's that funny noise then? *Boom-boom-boom-boom.* Then I realize. It's my heart beating.

6

I turn one way—there's a white wall. I turn another way—white wall again.

I can still see the sun. It's that pale lemon smudge high up in the fog. I can see my shadow on the sand. When I hold out my hand I can see that too. But after that it's a white candy-floss world. Haven't got a clue which way to go.

The sea's growling somewhere very close . . .

Then I panic and go charging through the fog. My feet are wet. There's foamy water sloshing round my shoes. And I realize I'm running in the wrong direction. I'm running out to sea.

'Can anybody hear me? Help! Help! I'm lost.'

My voice comes echoing back: *lost, lost, lost* . . .

Seaweed goes *pop pop pop!* under my shoes. It sounds loud as gunfire. But it means I'm out of the waves. I'm on dry sand again.

I make myself stop and listen. *Shhhh*, heart, stop going frantic!

Just a dead hush. I can't even hear the sea.

What's that? That blurry red thing over there? It's coming closer, swimming through the fog like a big red fish.

Whump, it was closer than I thought. I've just crashed into it.

'Ow!' it says.

'Stevie?'

It isn't him. It's one of those island kids, wearing a bright red T-shirt.

I wouldn't ask them for help. Not normally. But I'm desperate so I grab this one by the arm: 'You know how to get out of this fog?'

For an answer, he opens his blue mouth and laughs at me. 'Ha ha ha.' I can't believe it. He's laughing like it's a game of hide and seek. Like we're having really great fun!

He shakes my arm off and dashes away.

'Wait!' I yell after him. 'Have you seen my brother Stevie?'

But he's gone.

The little creep's gone. He's left me. Deliberately left me inside the fog.

It's so hot in here, hot as a greenhouse. But there's sparkly dewdrops all over me. On my fuzzy jumper, in my hair, even on my eyelashes. It's like trying to see through rainbows. I blink them away.

'Is anybody here?' My voice sounds strange, like it's not me talking. 'Is anybody here?'

Only my shadow, flapping about like a trapped bird.

And somewhere, very close, there's the sea.

Then, suddenly, the fog parts like curtains. There's a way out! I can see beach and the sea crystal clear. I start running for the gap but it slides shut like it's teasing me. I saw something though, before it closed again. I saw a woman down by the sea. She had long blue hair. I swear it, like a blue waterfall. I can't see anything now. No blue-haired woman. Just a white wall. I must be going crazy.

Then my foot slips. The ground underneath me crumbles away like cake. And suddenly I'm sliding down a sandbank towards deep, bubbling water . . .

'Help me!'

Someone grabs my coat, hauls me back up the sandbank. Then takes my hand and pulls me along like they're leading a little child.

Then, *plop*, I'm out of the fog into bright, bright sunlight.

It dazzles me. Makes me screw up my eyes. Then I open them a crack and see Stevie.

He's just standing there, with his two island friends, as if nothing at all has happened. He's so casual he's chewing gum. Then I realize from his blue lips that it's not gum. It's skyberries.

The first thing I think is: Phew, thank God he's safe.

Then I ignore him and go stomping up to the little creep who left me in the fog, probably to drown.

I've stopped being scared and I'm angry instead. I mean, really, really angry.

'What you playing at?' I'm screeching at this island kid. 'Why'd you leave me in there when you knew the way out?' I'm jabbing my finger in his chest, pushing him backwards. 'I nearly didn't get out. I didn't know which way to go. I nearly drowned!'

I thought these island kids might be brainless but this one is worse than all the rest. He's brain-dead! He just stares at me, with his blue mouth hanging open like he doesn't have a clue what language I'm speaking. For a minute I think I've got the wrong kid—I mean, they all look the same. But I can't have done because he's the one with the T-shirt that looked like a red fish in the fog.

'You did it deliberately, didn't you? You were even laughing!'

I stop pushing him. There's no point to it. I could push him all the way across the island and he wouldn't push back. On Pilot Island they're gentle people. That's what Mum told me. They farm oyster beds and catch lobsters and go fishing in the estuary. They just want the outside world to leave them alone. That's what Mum said. They're peace-loving people.

But I don't feel very peace-loving at the moment. It's that stupid puppy grin that gets me. As if he doesn't know what he just did.

'You laughing at me?' I ask Red Fish in my scariest voice. I can be really scary when I feel like it. The bullies that picked on Stevie used to run like mad when they saw me.

But Red Fish doesn't look scared, he looks confused. And he keeps peeping sideways at Stevie as if to say: 'Who is this crazy person?'

And Stevie says, 'What's wrong with you, Rach? What you getting so mad about? You weren't lost in there, were you? *Naaa!* Come on!'

And he smiles at his freaky little green-eyed mates, like they share some kind of important secret.

'*Naaa* yourself, Stevie! 'Course I was lost in there. You're not telling me that you found your way out of that fog? You couldn't find your way out of a paper bag!'

I didn't mean to say that. It's not Stevie's fault—the psychologist said so. I shouldn't have said it in front of the island kids. It just slipped out somehow.

But Stevie shrugs. 'I wasn't lost. I knew which way to go. I just knew.'

He sounds really calm and in control. That's not like Stevie. He gets hyper trying to handle a knife and fork.

Instead, I'm the one losing my cool. I mean, what's going on? It's like *they're* waiting for *me* to explain!

'I could have been killed back there!' is all I can think of to say.

I jerk my head towards the fog. It's already going away. Shrinking up the beach like it's being sucked back into the dunes.

And they just stand there grinning, even Stevie, as if I'm telling them a funny story.

'Course, I'm jumping by now, so mad I'm bursting. 'I'm glad you think it's a good laugh. Leaving someone to get drowned—deliberately! I'm glad you think it's a big joke. 'Cos I don't!'

Then this other voice comes from behind me: 'They didn't do it deliberately.'

I whirl around. 'What's it got to do with you?'

It's another of them—the island kids. Tall and skinny with wild black hair and green eyes. But this one is older than the other two. He's older than me even, about fifteen.

'I'm Alban,' he says, as if that's an answer. 'I came into the fog, got you out.'

'Oh.'

Suppose I should say thanks. But I'm still in a bad mood. All those seawater green eyes staring at me. Those skyberry mouths grinning as if I'm making a big fuss about nothing.

And anyway, what kind of a name is Alban? He looks a mess. He's wearing rolled-up corduroy trousers and an orange jumper—the same kind of jumble sale clothes they all wear.

'They didn't do it deliberately,' this Alban kid tells me again in a soothing voice like he's trying to calm down a snappy dog. 'They just didn't understand.'

'What's to understand? I was lost in there! Everyone gets lost in fog!'

Alban doesn't say anything.

'Well, don't they?'

He still doesn't agree. Even Stevie doesn't back me up. He just stares at me, like the others, as if I've got three heads or something. And I'm getting this very peculiar feeling that I'm alone with a bunch of aliens. Only they don't think they're aliens. They think I am.

The feeling gets worse when one of the island boys pipes up. It's Red Fish. He's not grinning now, he's frowning.

'Can't she home then?' he asks Alban as if he can hardly believe it.

Alban crouches down next to Red Fish. I can only hear some of what he says because he's whispering. '. . . told you, didn't I? She's from the mainland . . . mainlanders can't home . . . in fog or in the dark, they get lost . . . can't find their way home.'

'Wow!' Red Fish's blue lips make a surprised 'O' shape.

The other little island kid has stopped grinning too. And he's looking at me as if he feels sorry for me. Like I'm a really sad person, like I'm *deprived* or something. Who does he think he is?

'Are you coming home, Stevie?'

Suddenly, I want to get him away from these island kids. I wonder if they've got some kind of hold on him. If they're scaring him or something.

But he doesn't seem scared. He seems happy. He gives them a cheery wave and says, 'Catch you later.'

Stevie walks back along the beach with me. The sun has burnt the fog away. You can see the whole of Pilot Island. Not that there's much to see. Just miles of sand dunes and yellow gorse bushes and skyberry bushes and rabbit holes and scrubby grass.

And birds of course. This place is famous, would you believe. Famous for its migrating birds. Big deal. But Dad gets all excited about it. Soon, Dad says, in September, you won't be able to see the sky for wings. The migrants will be here. They come to feed on skyberries, Dad says. To fill up on them before they fly to Africa or somewhere else that's warm.

The two little kids and Alban are walking off to where they live. They look trembly in the hot sun, like a mirage. The island people live over the other side of the island. They live inside a high wall, to keep mainlanders like me out.

'You ever been in there?' I ask Stevie. 'Inside where they live?'

'Sure,' says Stevie. But his lips are tight. He doesn't want to say too much. And I get that creepy feeling again. That he knows things that I don't.

'Do you like it here, Stevie? On Pilot Island?'

He didn't like it on the mainland. He hated school. He couldn't write properly. He had no friends. He didn't fit in. When he couldn't do things, he threw a wobbly and banged his head on the wall. I was the only one who could calm him down. He used to talk to me.

But he isn't talking to me any more.

'Sure,' is all he says, shrugging.

'Why do you like it? It's horrible here, Stevie. There's nothing to do and it's just wind and sand and sea—and fog. You can't hardly see where you're going! And those kids—they're just freaky. What were they talking about back there? All that stuff about mainlanders can't home?'

'You wouldn't understand,' says Stevie, with a secretive little smile.

That really gets on my nerves. What a cheek, telling me I don't *understand*—when he can't even tie up his shoes!

'I can't believe you really like this place.'

'Yes I do,' says Stevie with that stubborn look he gets. 'I think it's great.'

'But why? Tell me a single good thing about it! It's like the bum-hole of the world!'

'I like it,' says Stevie, 'because I always know where I am. I don't get muddled up here, I don't get scared. I always know the way to go.'

'Eh? What you mean, always know the way to go?'

And what's he mean, 'don't get scared'? Pilot Island makes me scared. I've just been scared out of my mind.

But he's closed his blue lips tight. He's not going to tell me anything else.

'And why are you eating skyberries? They're crap. They leave this horrible taste in your mouth, like rusty old nails or something.'

I break off a piece of chocolate and hold it out to Stevie. 'Have some chocolate instead.' It's his favourite, with the peppermint bubbles inside.

'No thanks, Rach,' he says. 'I like skyberries better.'

I just stare at him, with my jaw nearly hitting my boots.

But to show me he isn't kidding he crams a handful of blue berries into his mouth and walks off towards the dunes. It's like a maze in there, a jungle of skyberries and thorny gorse bushes and twisty creeping plants with big, white flowers like floppy trumpets.

'You'll get lost, Stevie!'

He'll get lost and then he'll get mad and then he'll panic and then I'll have to go and rescue him.

'You'll get lost, you know you will. You don't know the way home,' I tell him sternly.

He turns round and stares at me. I call it his shark stare because his eyes look at you and never blink. And I think, I've done it now. I've upset him now. He's really mad now. That's always the first sign, when he stares at you like that.

He clenches up his fist and starts punching the air and I'm thinking, Back off, Rach, he's going to throw a wobbly!

I'm sure he is because now he's scowling and showing me his fist. He says, 'See this bunch of . . . '

And then he does something incredible.

He *doesn't* throw a wobbly.

Instead he unclenches his fist and spreads his fingers

14

wide and waggles them at me and says, 'Bunch of . . .
flowers!'

And he bows and grins, like a magician who's just done
a really amazing trick.

Then he sticks out his blue tongue at me and, still
grinning, disappears into the dunes.

2

'Mum! Come here a minute!'

'What's the matter?' Mum's heard me yelling and she's running upstairs.

'I'm here, Mum, in Stevie's bedroom.'

'This had better be important, Rachel,' Mum says, as she comes in the door. 'I'm going down to the schoolhouse. I've got some cupboards to clean out.'

I forgot to say, my mum's got a job here, as well as my dad. She's the new teacher, in the island school.

'So?' says Mum, impatiently. 'What did you call me for?'

'Did you tidy up in here?' I ask her. Every so often she goes berserk and attacks Stevie's room and shovels all his stuff into binbags.

'Nope. Wasn't me. I haven't had the time.'

'Well, look how tidy it is!'

Stevie's room is so neat it would win a neatness competition.

Now she's in here Mum is as amazed as I am. 'I can't believe it!' she says. But I'm worried too. And Mum doesn't seem worried at all.

'It's wonderful!' she says. 'This island is so good for Stevie. Haven't you noticed, Rach? He hardly ever loses his temper here.'

They think some kind of miracle's happened. And they won't listen to me. They want to believe the miracle.

'But look at it, Mum. I mean, this isn't just *normal* neatness, is it? This bedroom is *weird*.'

I don't know why it's weird. It just is. I liked it better when it was a wreck.

Stevie's shoes were always chucked in a heap. Now they're side by side, with the toes towards the window, as if they're on parade. He's set out his pencils in neat rows on his desk. And they point towards the window too. His model cars and tanks and planes and soldiers are arranged the same way. Everything lined up, exactly parallel, facing the window. It's like he's measured it with a ruler. As if he was making a deliberate pattern. As if it means something.

Suddenly, my skin starts to crawl. I don't like this. This is spooky.

'Don't be stupid, Rach,' I tell myself. 'It's only Stevie's bedroom.'

'Don't move that!'

I snatch my fingers back. Stevie comes rushing in and straightens up a pencil I just moved. I only moved it a millimetre.

'Don't move anything!' he says. 'Everything has got to be exactly . . . like . . . this.'

His lips are bright blue—he's been eating skyberries again. There's a dribble of blue juice down his chin.

'This is fantastic,' Mum gushes. Anything that Stevie does right is always fantastic. They always go way over the top. The day he learned to use scissors they put the flags out. Surprised they didn't put it in flashing lights on the front of the house. Like, announce it to the world. 'STEVIE USED A PAIR OF SCISSORS!'

'This is fantastic, Stevie.' Mum waves her arm around the room. 'You're really trying hard. You've really changed since we came to Pilot Island.'

He's changed all right. He's not like *our* Stevie any more. So why does she sound so pleased about it?

Stevie ignores her. He rushes over to his bed and starts trying to drag it along.

'What are you doing?' asks Mum.

'I don't want my bed here,' says Stevie. 'I want it the other way round.'

'Why?'

'Just . . . help . . . me . . . shift . . . this . . . bed,' Stevie gasps. 'I can't sleep this way round no more. It doesn't feel right.'

Mum laughs and shrugs, as if it's all a game. 'OK, if that's what you want. Let's give him a hand, Rach.'

'What you talking about, doesn't *feel* right?' I ask Stevie.

He doesn't say anything. He just stares at me, like Red Fish did, as if I'm a really pathetic person. As if I shouldn't need to ask such stupid questions.

I'm a bit shocked because Stevie never stared at me like that before. I don't want to sound boasting, but he always sort of looked up to me on the mainland.

So we start moving the bed.

'Ow!' I've crushed my little finger between the bed and the wall. It hurts like mad. I have to shake it about to stop it stinging.

'This bed's not in the right place,' Stevie complains.

'What's wrong with it?' I'm getting really irritated because my finger's throbbing. 'It's the other way round, isn't it?'

'But it's not in the right place yet.'

He tries to push the bed on his own. 'Move, you bed,' he tells it. There's a strange gleam in his eyes, like he's never going to give up, like it really matters to him.

'OK, OK,' says Mum. 'Stop it, you'll hurt yourself. We'll help you. Just tell us how it should be.'

She always gives in to Stevie.

So we drag that stupid bed until it's just where he wants it, down the middle of the room, with the bedhead under the window.

And still Stevie fusses, 'That's not right. It's got to be *straight.*' So we bump the bed a tiny bit this way, a tiny bit that way and I'm thinking, I'm going to thump him any minute *now*.

When suddenly he throws himself on the bed. He stretches out, lies still as a log and closes his eyes tight.

A little cold shiver goes crinkling down my spine. Because I've just noticed something. Stevie's made himself part of the pattern. He's lined himself up with the pencils, the cars, and all his other stuff. As if everything's *got* to be parallel and facing in the same direction. Even him.

Then he springs up again like a jack-in-the-box.

'That *feels* just right,' he says. He sounds really pleased. 'That's *excellent* for sleeping in now.'

'I think you're messing us about,' I tell him, in my most dangerous voice. 'Why are you so fussy all of a sudden? About your bedroom being arranged exactly right? It was a dump before and you never even noticed!'

I sound angry but I'm scared really. I understood Stevie before. All right, he was a pain in the neck sometimes. But I understood it when he threw a wobbly because of things he couldn't do. Now he's stopped throwing wobblies. And I haven't got a clue what's going on in his head.

Mum flashes me a warning look. I know that look. She uses it a lot. It means: 'Careful. We mustn't upset Stevie.'

'Well,' she says in a bright, chirpy voice, 'well, I think it's wonderful Stevie's being so tidy.'

And I have to bite my lip and say nothing.

Stevie doesn't thank us for moving the bed, even though I've practically broken my finger.

'I'm going out,' he says. 'Out with my friends.'

19

Mum doesn't look worried when he says this. Her face lights up, as if she's been given a really great present.

She just takes a quick look out the window. 'OK,' she says. 'You can go. There's no fog out there.'

'The fog can't hurt me anyway,' says Stevie. 'It only hurts mainlanders.'

And Mum doesn't even think that's a strange thing to say! She just isn't suspicious at all.

But I am. So, after I hear the front door slam I turn to Mum and say, 'Something's wrong with him. I know it is.'

What Mum does next really shocks me. She covers up her ears!

'No, Rachel,' she says. 'You don't know anything of the sort. I don't want to hear it. I know you don't like it here. But it's great for Stevie. He's even got friends here. Remember how I used to worry about him not making friends? He's a different boy on Pilot Island.'

I open my mouth to say, 'That's what I'm trying to tell you,' but she sounds so fierce and she's talking so fast that I daren't interrupt her. Besides, there's no point because she's still got her hands over her ears. So I just have to stand there and take it.

'He's confident now, sure of himself. He's calmed down a lot. He's even getting organized—just look at how he's tidied this room. Your dad and me can hardly believe how much he's changed. He's safe here, he's happy. I don't have to worry any more. And that's great because, to be honest, I got sick of worrying. So don't try and spoil it for us all, Rachel. Because I'm just not going to listen!'

I can't believe it. She's making me sound selfish when I'm just trying to warn her about Stevie.

'But, Mum!'

'I can't hear you!' she says.

20

She only takes her hands away when she's sure that my lips aren't moving.

She looks a bit shocked that she yelled her head off. I'm shocked too because my mum's a sweet person really. She hardly ever gets in a rage.

Then she starts being sorry about it. 'Look, Rachel,' she says. 'I didn't mean to shout. I just want the best for Stevie, that's all.'

I want to say, 'What about me? What about what's best for me?' But I can't say that because it sounds selfish and it's not Stevie's fault he's like he is.

Suppose I'd better explain about Stevie. He's dyspraxic. Yeah, I didn't know what it meant either. There are lots of reports on him by *occupational therapists* and *educational psychologists* and other people with tongue-twisting names. I haven't read them but Mum keeps them all in this thick file called 'STEVIE'S FILE'.

Anyway, being dyspraxic means he's more clumsy than other kids. I mean, *much* more clumsy. He's got *no* co-ordination, no sense of direction. His writing's crap—it takes him forever to write just a few lines. He can't swim or ride a bike or play football like other kids. Sometimes his hands and feet won't do what he tells them. He tells his feet, 'Walk round this stone!' and they just go Thwack! straight into it. He tells his hand, 'Put this cup on the table!' and the cup misses the table and smashes on the floor.

There's lots more about it—about 'motor learning difficulties' and 'hand/eye co-ordination' and 'behavioural problems' that I don't know how to explain. But, imagine this: You can't write down the answers even though, inside your head, you know them all. You can't catch a ball even though, inside your head, you're a star goalie. That's what it's like for Stevie. OK?

I know all this stuff about Stevie off by heart. I'm an expert on it. I could pass an exam on it. I've listened to Mum and Dad going on and on about Stevie's problems for hours and hours and hours.

Mum's already pulled on her rubber gloves and gone back downstairs to do the washing up.

'When's our wind turbine coming? When can I play my CDs?' I shout after her. I know the answer already but I feel like being awkward. Why shouldn't I be? They should feel guilty I'm so miserable.

'I told you a million times—on Monday,' she calls up the stairs. She doesn't sound very guilty.

'Monday! We don't get electricity until *Monday*! That's ages to wait!'

I scowl out the window.

It's low tide. The sea is a smudgy grey line on the horizon. The estuary's full of smooth wet sand and rock pools and all these silver snakes. They're not silver snakes really. They're rivers of seawater, left behind when the tide went out.

'What a dump.'

It's not even a proper island because at low tide, like now, you can walk across the estuary to the mainland. It's about a mile. There are long poles stuck in the sand to show you where it's safe to walk. Half-way along the line of poles, stuck in the middle of the estuary, is what looks like a tree-house on stilts.

When I first saw it, I asked Dad, 'What's a tree-house doing out there?'

He said, 'You mean, that little wooden hut on legs? It's a *tidal refuge*, Rach. See that ladder going up to it? You climb up there if you're walking across the sand and get trapped by the tide.'

But there's no one walking across the sand. Why would

22

there be? No one wants to come here. And anyway, you need a special permit because it's a wild life reserve.

And the islanders never go to the mainland. They row across in their boats sometimes and pick up stuff they need from the jetty. But that's as far as they go. Like I said before, island life: GOOD; mainland life: BAD. That's what they think. Well, I think what they think is rubbish.

Wait a minute. Who's that?

There *is* someone out there. It's a tiny figure all on its own out by the refuge. All I can see is its back. But it's got long, blue hair.

It's that woman again. The one I saw in the fog. She's for real, I did see her. The fog wasn't playing tricks on me. She's out there walking along by the poles. Escaping from Pilot Island and heading for the mainland.

3

You can see the whole of Pilot Island from where I'm standing. There's our new house over there, all sparkling white. And over there, behind those high walls, is where the islanders live. There are about a hundred of them, Dad says. But you can't see what they do inside. You can only see them creeping in and out of the gates. Going to the oyster beds or to their fishing boats down on the beach. They look like big birds, like herons or something—all tall and thin and stooping with their long noses.

Mum thinks the sun shines out of their backsides. 'I respect them,' she says. 'They're such gentle, humble fisher-folk.'

Humble, my bottom. They think they're special. They think they're better than anyone else.

'We have a lot to learn from their simple way of life,' my mum says.

She talks like that sometimes. She can't help it. She's a teacher, remember.

I wonder where Stevie is. I wonder if he's inside the walls, with Red Fish, or Alban. He spends all his time now with the islanders. These days, I hardly see him. He just says, 'Hi, Rach. Bye, Rach,' and he's out the door.

I know where Mum is. She's at the schoolhouse sorting things out.

I can see the schoolhouse from here. It's a school hut really. It's got a tin roof that flashes in the sun. It's about half-way between our house and where the islanders live. 'There are only eighteen children in the school,' my mum told me. 'So we'll be one big happy family.'

Count me out. Stevie's going to go there. But I'm not. No way, I told Mum and Dad. No way I'm going to school in some crap little hut with a tin roof. Where there's only one room with an old iron stove to heat it. Where seagulls go *squawk!* past the windows and my mum's the only teacher.

So in September I'm going back to my old school, Parkview High, where all my friends are. Dad's taking me in the jeep. He'll drive it across to the mainland. And if the tides aren't right and I can't get back to Pilot Island (what a shame!) I'm staying with my friend Sophie. My mum's arranged it all with her mum. I'm going to sleep on the top bunk in Sophie's bedroom. It'll be really good fun.

So that's why I'm not going completely crazy here. You might have wondered that—why I'm not banging my head off walls like Stevie used to. It's because I'm not stuck here forever. I'll be back on the mainland soon with *normal* people.

And on Monday they're fixing up our wind turbine so I can watch telly and listen to my music. So it doesn't matter if those island kids want to ignore me, if they treat me like I don't exist. Who needs them?

I don't need them. I'm going exploring now, on my own. Actually, I've got some music with me. I'm humming along to it because I've got my earphones on and my personal stereo hooked to my belt. So I don't feel lonely at all.

I can spy on the whole of Pilot Island from on top of this sand dune. I feel like King of the Castle.

There's Dad over there, by our house. He's crawling around in the skyberry bushes, studying rabbits.

He's been doing a lot of that lately, watching rabbits. He says he's never seen anything like the rabbits on Pilot

Island. He says they've got some very strange behaviour patterns. Don't ask me what he's talking about. They just look like any old rabbits to me. (Except they've got bright blue poo from eating skyberries—just thought you'd like to know that.)

Anyway, over there is where I'm going exploring. I've seen nearly all of the island, except inside the walls of course. But the other part I haven't seen is a rocky bit that sticks out into the sea. It's only a little rocky bit but it's got a name. Wreckers' Point, it's called.

'Time you went to check out Wreckers' Point, Rach,' I tell myself as I go sliding down the dune.

Must stop that—talking to myself. I seem to be doing a lot of that lately.

Even Pilot Island looks OK today. The sun's shining, the sky's blue, the sea's sparkly and I'm walking round to Wreckers' Point humming to myself when I walk slap-bang into a house.

I'm so surprised that I turn off my music and push the headphones down round my neck.

It was only a little house but it's a wreck now. There's no roof, it's wide-open to the sky. The walls are black and crumbly as burnt toast.

A salty wind is blowing through the living room. *Squawk!* A seagull zooms in one window, out another.

Scattered about is all this cindery, burnt-out junk. I can't tell what it used to be. I kick out at a rusty box. It goes *clang* and the front falls open. Then I recognize what it used to be. It used to be a microwave oven.

Questions start jumping about in my brain: Whose house was this? Who needs a microwave oven when there's no electricity?

I bet none of the islanders have ever heard of microwave ovens.

26

Questions are still hitting me *blam, blam, blam,* when I hear seashells crunching behind me. Someone's coming.

I whirl around. 'Dad!'

'Sorry, did I scare you, Rach? I didn't mean to.'

He climbs over some rubble to get into the house.

'Dad, what is this place? Did you know it was here? Who lived here?'

My dad has always been a far-away sort of person. You know, like he's not there most of the time. Even on the mainland, when he worked for the Wildlife Trust, it was really hard to get his attention.

His eyes mostly look sort of dreamy, like he's thinking about something else. And he probably is. He's probably thinking about rabbits.

Since we came to Pilot Island he's been rabbit crazy. There's no point trying to talk to him. He spends all his time wandering round in the sand dunes, making notes on his computer. It's a dinky little thing, Dad's computer. It's got a keyboard and screen like a big PC but it runs on batteries and it folds up and fits right into your pocket. I want one for Christmas.

'Dad? Are you listening?'

He snaps his computer shut and slides it into his pocket.

'Dad, do you know who lived here?'

That microwave oven is really bothering me. What's it doing here?

Suddenly, my dad doesn't look vague any more. He looks shifty. That surprises me because my dad's not a shifty person.

'Err,' he says, 'errrr . . . '

'You do know, don't you, Dad?'

He gives this quick grin, like I've caught him out, and says, 'It used to be the warden's house.'

'What warden? You're the warden.'

'The one before me.'

'Oh.'

I didn't know there was a warden before Dad. I didn't even think about it.

'What happened to his house?'

'It got burnt down,' says Dad.

'No, you're kidding me!' (I'm using my sarcastic voice.)

I tap a burnt book with my foot. It just sort of *dissolves* into a pile of dust. Then the wind blows the dust out the door.

Dad shrugs, 'Well, that's all I know. There was some kind of accident and this cottage got burnt down. That's why they built a brand new warden's house.'

'He had a microwave,' I tell Dad, jerking my thumb towards the rusty box. 'What's he want that for?'

'Actually,' Dad says, 'it was a woman. The warden before me was a young woman. From the mainland, like us.'

'Well, what did *she* want it for then?'

'She had electricity. She had her own generator,' Dad says. 'Like we're going to have.'

'Huh! Well, she was lucky. At least she could have some Micro Chips. At least she could dry her hair.'

'She wasn't all that lucky,' says Dad.

The way his voice sounds—strange and serious—makes me really uneasy. 'Why? What happened to her? Did she get hurt in the fire? She didn't get killed or anything did she?'

Dad looks uncomfortable, like he doesn't want to tell me. Then he shakes his head and says, 'She got drowned. Out there, in the estuary.'

'Drowned?'

When he says the word *drowned* I'm suddenly shivering like the temperature's dropped below zero. I can't help it. I can't help staring at the estuary. The tide's going out. There's just grey, smelly mud out there, miles and miles of it. It's got a horrible shiny skin, like the skin of poison tree frogs. You can sink in that mud, if you don't keep to the path by the poles.

'How did this warden person get drowned?'

'I don't know much about it,' Dad says. 'Just what I read in the newspapers—oh, over a year ago.'

I can't remember reading anything in the newspapers. But then I don't read the papers much. And even if I'd read it I wouldn't have taken any notice. A year ago Pilot Island was just a name.

'Well, the papers said it was a tragic accident. That a fire started and she probably panicked and ran out of the house to escape. But there was a really bad fog that night and she ran the wrong way . . . '

'She ran out to sea.'

'Must have done. They found her washed up along the coast a few days later.'

My eyes are closed now. I'm remembering when I got lost in the fog. I know how that warden felt. When the waves started creeping round her ankles and she knew she was heading in the wrong direction.

She must have known what the tide is like here. How it races in and cuts you off and then drowns you really slowly, taking its time. She must have known she didn't stand a chance. I'm remembering running this way, that way, flapping about in the fog like a trapped bird. And I'm panicking just *thinking* about it . . .

'Are you all right, Rach?'

I open my eyes again. I'm angry with Dad, I don't know why. 'You kept pretty quiet about all this, didn't you? About the warden before you? About her house burning down? About her running away and getting drowned?'

Dad looks embarrassed. 'Well, it wasn't a secret or anything. It was in all the papers. I thought you knew. And anyway, it's not the sort of thing you want to talk about, is it, when you're moving to a new place?'

'You mean it'd be bad luck, talking about how the last warden got drowned?'

Dad gives a shrug. 'Something like that.'

But he's already lost interest in the last warden. His eyes have got that dreamy look and he's flipping open his little computer again.

'You know, Rach,' he says, 'Pilot Island is a very strange place. A very strange place indeed.'

'You don't have to tell me that.'

'I mean, the way the animals behave. I've never seen anything like it. Today, just along from our house, the sea's washed the top off a sand dune—there must have been a very big wave or something. Anyway, it's just sliced the top off and you can see the rabbit burrows underneath. It's really strange—'

'It's not the rabbits that are strange,' I interrupt him. 'It's the people. Or haven't you noticed? And Stevie's getting just like them.'

But Dad carries on talking about the rabbits.

'These rabbit burrows, Rach—they're amazing. They dig them all in the same direction from north to south. In exactly parallel lines. They must do it deliberately. It's so *precise*. It couldn't just be chance.'

I'm making connections. 'Course I am. Thinking straightaway about Stevie's room and how precise that is and how he's gone crazy for parallels.

'Dad?'

But he's wandered off. Out of the burnt-out house that belonged to the last warden. And off among the sand dunes. He's thinking about those rabbits. The ones with the bright blue bunny poo that dig parallel burrows.

You don't have to tell me about this place being weird.

And I haven't even told him yet about the blue-haired woman.

4

I've almost made up my mind not to go exploring on Wreckers' Point. The sun's still out. The sea's still sparkly. But the day seems to be darker somehow, since Dad told me about the last warden. I keep seeing her struggling in the estuary while her house burns down and the cold salty waves go *slosh, slosh* into her mouth.

She might have been really close to the beach and safety. Only a few metres away. But she was a mainlander like me. So she couldn't find her way back.

Mainlanders can't home. Mainlanders can't home. What Alban said keeps flashing up in my brain.

But *islanders* can home. They always seem to know their way. They take their fishing boats out at night. In the pitch black. With no radar or compasses or anything. Dad says so. He says it's amazing, they're natural navigators. Even in the fog and dark.

So why didn't they rescue her then?

Someone must have seen her house burning. Why didn't they rescue her like Alban rescued me?

Wonder what her name was? Wonder what she looked like?

But I don't really want to know anything about her. That would make it too personal.

'Stop it, Rachel!' That's me, telling myself off. I have to shake my head like a wet dog to drive out those gloomy questions.

But I'm still shivering, like someone's walking over my grave.

I put my headphones back on and turn the music up

really loud, *boom, boom, boom, boom,* so it rattles my brains. That's better.

Not long now, Rach, is what I'm thinking. Not long now—just until September 5th—and you'll be out of this madhouse. You'll be back on the *mainland,* where things are *normal.*

'Mainland *good,* island *bad*! Mainland *good,* island *bad*!'

I know it's stupid, screaming that out loud. But it chases the dark shadows away.

Might as well carry on to Wreckers' Point. You can see it from here—a sort of grey finger of rock curving out into the estuary. There's a building on the end of it. What is it? Some kind of tower? If it is, it's fallen down, because there's only a bit of it left. I can't make it out. Should have brought Dad's binoculars.

So I trudge along, chanting, 'Mainland *good,* island *bad*! Mainland good, island *mad*!' when, suddenly, I come over the top of a dune and I'm there.

And the first thing I see is the blue-haired woman. She's far out on Wreckers' Point. She's not looking in my direction. She's staring out to sea. And her hair is spread over her back like a blue waterfall.

I creep closer and closer, holding my breath. I'm out on the rocks now. There's no way she can hear my music but I switch it off as if it might scare her away. She looks really strange with her blue hair, sitting beside a ruined tower. Like some figure out of a fantasy game.

She's turning round!

She's looking straight at me, with this long, cool stare. She doesn't seem surprised to see me. It's like she knew I was there all the time. The shock makes me hiss through my teeth. 'Ssssss.'

'Course, she isn't a fantasy figure. Her face is creased

33

like an old paper bag. 'She's just some old woman,' I tell myself.

Except she's got wild blue hair.

But that hair doesn't fool me. She's one of them all right. Even if I saw her heading for the mainland she's still one of them. She's got the island face—green seawater eyes and a long nose. And she can home, can't she? The first time I ever saw her she was mooching around in the fog.

But even if she didn't have that island face I'd still know she was one of them. It's the way they look at you if you're a mainlander. Not friendly or unfriendly. Just like you don't matter.

'Hello!' someone yells. Who's that? I whirl around. It's Alban. He comes scrambling up to Wreckers' Point from somewhere down on the beach.

And it's funny but I'm quite pleased to see him because next to her he seems quite normal. Even his blue skyberry lips don't spook me—much.

He yells out something to the old woman but I can't hear him very well because I've still got my earphones on. I push them off my head as he yells out again.

'Hello, Mistress Lodesman!'

I heard that all right.

She heard it too and gets up and comes walking back from the ruined tower. She doesn't move like she's old. She's springy, like a deer. Her bare arms and legs are wiry and brown.

Alban says, 'Hello,' to me. About time. I was beginning to think I didn't exist. I get that feeling a lot on Pilot Island.

He's got a sack filled with something and a bundle of wood under his arm. When she gets near he opens the sack up to show her. It looks like it's full of blue jewels.

'Skyberries for you, Mistress Lodesman,' he says. 'And some driftwood for your stove.'

She's wearing this flappy grey dress. And leather sandals that make her brown feet look like big goblin feet. The sandals go slap, slap, slap on the rock of Wreckers' Point. The dress looks like it's been made from an old blanket. How could I mistake her for a fantasy princess?

'You're a good boy, Alban,' she says, raking around in the berries.

Her voice is a big surprise. She sounds like a teacher. You know, the way she says, 'You're a good boy, Alban.' You can always tell.

'This is Stevie's sister,' Alban tells her, nodding in my direction.

It's pitiful because I'm grateful they've noticed me. I mean, really grateful. But at the same time I hate it when he calls me, 'Stevie's sister'. As if Stevie's the person that matters. And I'm just his shadow or something.

Anyway, this Mistress Lodesman gives me a quick, cool nod. She's not exactly falling over herself to be friendly. Didn't expect her to. They're all the same. Except for Alban. He talks more than the rest of them. And, big surprise, he even wants to talk to me.

'Mistress Lodesman makes our skyberry wine,' he tells me. 'And she makes skyberry juice for the babies.'

He slings the sack over his shoulder. 'I'll take these things up to your house for you, Mistress Lodesman.'

I didn't see any house. But I can see it now. It's back there, overlooking the sea. It's a little low cottage. No wonder I missed it—it's made from the same grey stone as Wreckers' Point. And it's got a mossy roof with sea lavender growing on it. You could walk straight past it and think it was part of the rock.

I don't know whether to follow Alban. I'm hanging

back feeling like I shouldn't be here, when he says, 'Come inside. Mistress Lodesman will not mind.'

She doesn't seem thrilled. Not thrilled at all. But Alban doesn't notice because he's already ducked inside her house.

What's that noise? That tinkling sound? There's a wind chime in the doorway. It's made of bits of glass—green, brown, and blue—washed smooth as pebbles by the sea.

'Come in!' Alban shouts, from inside.

Mistress Lodesman nods at me to go in. But her lips are tight. I've just noticed—her lips aren't blue. They're pink like mine. Why aren't her lips blue, like all the other islanders?

'Where are you?' Alban pokes his head out the door and beckons me inside.

There's something shining inside Mistress Lodesman's cottage. Like blue crystals in a dark cave.

When I step inside I realize it's rows of bottles and jars. They're on the floor, on shelves round the walls. And they've all got blue stuff inside.

'Skyberry wine,' says Alban. 'Skyberry juice. Bottled skyberries. Skyberry vinegar.'

It takes a while for my eyes to get used to the dark.

'Does she make all this then?'

Who said that? It was me. I didn't recognize my own voice for a minute. It seems like ages since I used it.

'Mistress Lodesman makes wine for the whole island,' says Alban. 'But she never drinks it herself. She doesn't like skyberries. Perhaps because she sees so many! She must be the only person here who doesn't like them.'

Except me, I'm thinking. But I'm only a mainlander, I don't count.

So that's why her lips aren't blue. It's because she never eats skyberries.

'She's got blue hair though,' I tell Alban just in case he hadn't noticed.

'It's white really. But she rinses her hair in skyberry vinegar,' says Alban, as if it's perfectly normal. 'She says it leaves it soft and shiny.'

'Oh, yeah, right,' is all I can say, as if I think it's perfectly normal too.

Then Mistress Lodesman comes in with her hair turned blue by skyberry vinegar and her pale pink, tight lips. And I daren't ask any more questions. Because Alban might not mind but I bet she does. She's got that look in her eyes. You know, that look some strict teachers have. That warn you not to mess them about.

But I'm bursting to ask questions. I really need to. Because this cottage is really strange. It's got skyberry wine bubbling away in the corners. And strings of them hanging like Christmas decorations from the ceiling. There's a blue glow everywhere you look.

But it's not just a skyberry factory. It's an office too. Didn't expect that. Not on Pilot Island where they live in the Dark Ages. I mean, you'd think they still used quill pens or carved things on stone or something. But there are filing cabinets in here—two green ones made of metal. And there's an office desk. It's got an oil lamp on it and piles of papers. And a dinky little fold-up computer. A bit like Dad's, except it's grey.

'That's like my dad's! Does it run off batteries too?'

Mistress Lodesman doesn't answer. Alban just nods. He's seen me staring but he doesn't say anything. As if he's a little bit scared of Mistress Lodesman too.

The computer was a big enough shock. But there's something else. I've got to ask about it. I've just got to. I mean, what's it doing here?

It's some kind of old uniform. Honest, that's what it

looks like. A blue uniform dripping with loads of gold trimming like it's a Christmas tree. Even the buttons are gold. It's very old, sort of antique. You can tell that straightaway. The cloth is musty and faded. But it's hanging on the wall as if it's dead important. Just hanging there, like it's a work of art or something.

'That's a funny thing to have on your wall. What is it?'

The way they look at each other I think I've asked something wrong, something that's not respectful. I can hear Mum's voice in my head: 'You've got to respect their way of life.'

But they tell me, anyway. And it's not even Alban this time. It's her, Mistress Lodesman.

'That is the uniform of an estuary pilot,' she says, as if she's really proud, 'of a Master Pilot. It's Asa Lodesman's uniform—my great-great-grandfather. That uniform is one hundred and fifty years old. I keep it to honour his memory. And this,' she says, nodding at the desk, 'is his very own brass telescope.'

I never noticed it before. But on the desk there's a telescope, polished to a golden shine.

'Oh, yeah. Right.'

I seem to be saying that a lot lately. I think Pilot Island is doing my head in. It's full of mysteries. I don't know what's going on.

There's a photo on the wall by the uniform. I peer at it, just to be polite.

It's old and cracked and yellowy. But there's this man staring out of it. He's sitting on a stool in front of a cottage and staring at me. He's not smiling. He's got a uniform on, the same as the one hanging on the wall. Except he's got a cap and a waistcoat to go with it. And he's got this amazing beard. It's long and grey and divided into two like a snake's forked tongue.

'That is my great-great-grandfather—Asa Lodesman himself,' Mistress Lodesman tells me before I even asked. 'It was taken not long before he died. Behind him is this cottage—where he lived all of his life.'

I never noticed it was the same cottage. I peer at the photo a bit closer.

'There are your wind chimes in the doorway! They must be really old!'

Mistress Lodesman nods, pleased that I've noticed.

'Was he a famous pilot, then?' I ask just for something to say.

There's another funny look, between her and Alban. Their green seawater eyes meet, just for a second. At least, I think they did. But maybe I'm getting too jumpy. Pilot Island makes you like that.

'He was,' she tells me in a solemn voice. 'He was a very great navigator. His name was known by the masters of every merchant vessel. From Japan, from the Baltic ports, from all over the world. He didn't need charts or landmarks. He could home in the thickest fog, the blackest night. There was no need for lightships in this estuary. Not when masters had Asa Lodesman to guide them in.'

She snaps her mouth shut, as if she's said too much. Then there's this embarrassing silence while we all stare at her great-great-grandad's pilot's uniform, hanging on the wall. The buttons wink back at us like golden eyes. Mistress Lodesman goes up and breathes on one of them and rubs it shiny on her dress. Tick, tick, tick. There's a clock somewhere. I just noticed it. Tick, tick, tick.

Alban speaks first.

'I have to go now, Mistress Lodesman. I have to help Dad with the fishing.'

She doesn't even seem to hear us.

So we back out of the cottage into the bright sunshine. Over our heads the glass pebbles go tinkle, tinkle.

Suddenly I'm sick of being respectful.

'Who's she then?' I asked Alban, jerking my thumb back towards the cottage. 'She seems a bit crazy if you ask me.'

He looks shocked. But he's found his tongue again. 'Mistress Lodesman isn't crazy,' he tells me. 'She used to be our school mistress before she retired and your mother came.'

Aha! I knew it. I knew she'd been a teacher. You can always tell. I feel pleased because at last I guessed something right about Pilot Island.

'Knew she was a teacher,' I tell Alban.

But then he spoils it.

'And she's our Go-Between,' he says.

I'm out of my depth again.

'What?'

'Our Go-Between—she goes between here and the mainland. Did you see in her cottage? She keeps the business accounts, from the fishing and the oyster beds. Often we need to deal with the mainland. It can't be avoided. So the Go-Between does it. She's a very important person.'

'I saw her! I saw her the other day from Stevie's bedroom window. She was walking across the estuary.'

He nods. 'She catches the bus into Lincoln. She will have had business there. Something to do for the islanders.'

'Wait a minute!' I've just remembered something. 'I thought you couldn't go to the mainland. I thought you got sick if you went there?'

'The Go-Between doesn't,' he says, as if it's obvious.

'Oh, yeah. Right. So why doesn't she live with the rest of you. Behind that wall?'

'She chooses not to. She chooses to live in Asa Lodesman's house.'

'Oh, right.'

We're going back a different way, climbing down from Wreckers' Point on to the beach. I can see that crumbly old ruin more clearly now. There's not much of it left. But it looks like some kind of tower, right out on the rocks, made out of massive blocks of stone.

'Was there some sort of castle out there?'

'A castle?'

'Yeah, that tower thing, out on the end of Wreckers' Point.'

Alban flicks his black hair out of his eyes. His hair's too long. It's like my dad's, like a shaggy dog. He needs a haircut.

'It wasn't a castle. It was a lighthouse.'

His green eyes look worried like it's something he doesn't want to talk about.

'A lighthouse? I never knew there was a lighthouse on Pilot Island. What happened to it? Did the sea knock it down?'

He shakes his head. 'There was a fire. That's what they say. They say the lighthouse keeper started it, by accident. It all happened a very long time ago.'

Then he's off, climbing down the seaweedy rocks. And I'm left high up on Wreckers' Point, with the salty wind in my face and the seagulls whirling round me like a snowstorm. I'm looking at the lighthouse—you can't tell it got burnt down. The stones are white as bones. But I'm thinking about that other place. The house that belonged to the poor drowned warden. That got burnt down too—by accident.

A queasy idea comes into my head.

'Hey,' I yell after Alban. 'What about this lighthouse keeper? Was he a mainlander? What happened to him?'

But Alban's way down on the beach. His voice comes floating back up. He's not saying anything about lighthouse keepers.

He's saying, 'Come down here, Rachel. Come and see Asa Lodesman's pilot boat!'

5

The climb down from Wreckers' Point is scary. I'm
watching my feet the whole time in case I slip. When
there's safe, crunchy sand under my shoes I can look
around again.

And I'm really surprised. I thought when Alban said
Asa Lodesman's boat he meant some piddly little boat like
you row around on a lake. But she's a wooden sailing
boat, much bigger than I thought—like a yacht or
something. She must be old but all her paint looks fresh.
As if Asa Lodesman had just put his paintbrush down.

'She's a pilot cutter,' says Alban. 'Built in 1850. Very
fast.'

He sounds proud of her. I don't know hardly anything
about boats but even I can see she's something special.
She's hauled high up on the beach, so the sea can't float
her away.

Her name's on the side in white letters: 'DOVE'. And
on the other side it says, 'A. LODESMAN. PILOT'. Soon
as I read his name I see that photo of him in my head.
With his long forked beard like Moses and his stern face.

'I've done a lot of work on her,' says Alban, 'to keep
her seaworthy.'

'Why is she painted black?'

I don't like black. She looks like a funeral ship or
something.

'Doves are white,' I tell Alban. 'She should be painted
white.'

'All the pilot cutters in the estuary had to be black then.
It was the law. And Mistress Lodesman likes her kept just

like she was when *he* sailed her. We've got the original sails. If we wanted we could sail her out to sea. And she would look just like she did in 1850.'

He stares across the estuary with dreamy eyes. As if he can see the *Dove* out on the silver water. And suddenly, I think I can see her too. A black *Dove* with all her sails up and flags flying. And grim old Asa in his pilot's uniform. Stomping round the deck. Spying out for ships through his brass telescope.

'Want to go on board?' Alban asks me. 'There's a ladder at the stern. She's perfect below decks too. There's a little iron stove they used to make the tea.'

'Er, got to get home,' I tell him, a bit too quickly.

He looks disappointed. But that's too bad. I don't want to go inside the *Dove*. Just thinking about climbing up those high black sides gives me the creeps.

'Let's go,' I tell him and we go crunching along the beach. The tide is coming in again and foamy waves are going slush, slush on to the sand.

I take a look over my shoulder. You can't see Mistress Lodesman's cottage any more. Or the *Dove* or even Wreckers' Point with its lighthouse that burnt down.

We're in the heart of the dunes now. In that dark wild wood of skyberry bushes and yellow gorse bushes that smell like coconut.

Every so often you have to leap little streams. They're fresh, not salty water. They come bubbling up from deep underground and gush down through the dunes to the sea.

And you have to watch out for rabbit holes. You could bust your ankle in one of those. I can't help remembering what Dad said—about the rabbits on Pilot Island digging their burrows north to south in dead straight lines. Wish I had X-ray eyes so I could look through the dunes and see them. See those bunny burrows all parallel, as neat as Stevie's bedroom.

But then something Alban says drives rabbits clean out of my head.

'What's it like on the mainland?' he asks me.

I'm so surprised that I just look bug-eyed and say, 'Pardon?'

There's a scoop of warm white sand in the grass. Alban sits down there and says, 'I've never been to the mainland. Tell me what it's like.'

He seems really desperate to know.

So I sit down next to him. 'Budge up.'

I've been thinking ever since we moved to Pilot Island, Mainland: GOOD. Pilot Island: BAD. But when he asks me, straight out like that, what it's like on the mainland, I have to give it some serious thought.

'Well . . . it's not boring on the mainland. There's always plenty to do.' That's not strictly true because I was bored quite a lot of the time. But I don't want him to know that. I want him to think the mainland is better than a million Pilot Islands.

And, like I said, he seems desperate to know. He's not snooty like the others. He's looking at me as if I'm a wise person with all the answers. So I have to make the mainland sound really good, don't I?

'It's great on the mainland. A zillion times better than it is here. Kids have loads of things to do. You can go ice skating, or go to the pictures, or to McDonald's, or rent a video, or just hang around with your mates. You can go shopping. I mean, when you go to buy sweets there's so many things to choose from. Not just skyberries like you have here. There's shelves and shelves of stuff! Like Mars Bars and Snickers—'

'Snickers?'

See, I said before that it was child cruelty. He doesn't even know what Snickers are. What's the point in telling him any more? He won't understand.

Then I have a brilliant idea. 'Look, Alban, why don't you come and see?'

There's another thing I said before. I said I didn't want anything to do with these Pilot Islanders. That I didn't need them. But Alban is different. He's all right. He's friendly and even quite good-looking if he gets his hair cut. I wouldn't mind taking him to the mainland.

The more I think about it, the more it seems like a great idea. I'm even quite excited about it.

'We could go tomorrow. We could go to the shopping mall.'

I've got loads of pocket money saved up—there's nothing to spend it on on Pilot Island.

He's obviously thinking it over. He gazes out over the estuary towards the mainland with this kind of restless, longing look in his eyes. 'I'd like to see it.'

But he's still chewing his blue lips. He's not sure yet because he says, 'Mistress Lodesman is the Go-Between. The rest of us only go as far as the jetty. The mainland isn't a good place for islanders. We get sick—'

'How do you know you get sick if you haven't been?'

He shrugs. 'Everyone here says so. Everyone knows it's true.'

'Oh, come on!'

I can't help sounding sneery. He's spoiling all my plans. 'Use your brains! Why should the mainland make you sick? It's just a stupid story. They're just control freaks, that's all. They want to keep you on Pilot Island. They know that if they let you go to the mainland, you'll never want to come back to this bumhole!'

I'm really keen to persuade him now. It matters a lot

to me. I hate those Pilot Islanders for telling their kids such stupid lies.

'They're brainwashing you! So you stay on Pilot Island and do the fishing and look after the oysters and be a good boy. So you work yourself to death and smell of lobsters all the time and never have any freedom.'

I feel really fired up. I haven't felt so fired up about anything since we moved here. It's like a personal mission. I'm going to rescue Alban, if it's the last thing I do.

Besides, they've got Stevie. They've made him into an islander. So I'm going to get my own back. I'm going to make Alban into a mainlander. They won't know him soon. When he gets some decent trainers and some designer clothes and uses a spray deodorant, they won't be able to tell him apart from any of the mainland boys. Except for those blue lips.

'Listen!' I switch on my personal stereo and tear the headphones from round my neck. 'This is the kind of music we listen to on the mainland. This is what we dance to.'

Before he can stop me I ram the headphones down over his ears and turn up the music loud.

'Good, isn't it?'

What's wrong with him? He's shaking his head like there are wasps in the earphones. Then, suddenly, he rips them off.

'Hey, careful! Those aren't mine!'

They're Stevie's actually. I borrowed them out of his bedroom this morning.

But Alban doesn't seem to be able to hear me. He jumps up and tries to run. But he doesn't get anywhere—he just staggers about. The razor grass is slicing his ankles. There's blood trickling down. But he doesn't even notice.

Then he crouches in the skyberry bushes rocking his head backwards and forwards in his hands. After a bit, he stops rocking. He takes his hands away from his head. He's OK. Phew, I was worried there for a minute.

'What's the matter? Don't you like the music? *Everybody* on the mainland likes that music! You've *got* to like it.'

I can see that I've got a lot of work to do, teaching him about what's cool and what's not.

'My head,' he says, looking dazed. 'My head.'

'Look, sorry,' I tell him. 'I turned the music up too loud. That's all it was. It does make your ears kind of buzz if you're not used to it. Is your head all right now?'

He concentrates hard, like he's tuning in to his own brainwaves. Then he says, 'Yes, it's all right now.'

So we carry on walking.

Suddenly, *Pow*, we break out of the dark skyberry jungle into brilliant sunshine.

Where are we? I know. There's the burnt-out cottage down there. The one that belonged to the poor last warden. I wanted to ask Alban about that. Ask him if he knew her or anything. But I've got more urgent questions on my mind.

'So, are we going to the mainland tomorrow? You'll like it. Honest, it's better than this place.'

He's thinking. They're all like that, this island lot, they think for a long time before they speak. It drives you crazy. *Meanwhile* I'm biting my fingernails and thinking, Say yes. Say yes. I've already planned out what we're going to do. I think I'll keep him away from my friends. Just until I've smartened him up a bit.

After thinking for *ages* he says, 'I should like to see the mainland with my own eyes.'

'Great!'

We arrange some details. He says he can row us over

48

but I don't like boats. They make me seasick, even the little ones.

So we decide to walk over at low tide.

'We'll have to wait until after the morning fog,' I warn him.

He looks puzzled for a second. 'Why?' he asks me. Then his face lights up and he says, 'Oh, sorry. I forgot that you can't home. It's all right. You can't get lost in the fog if you're with me.'

I don't like him saying that. It makes me sound like a baby—as if I can only reach the mainland by holding his hand through the fog. But I don't say anything. He might change his mind about going. And I've got my heart set on it now.

'We'd better go in the fog,' he says. 'Then no one will see us.'

'Will they try to stop you?' I can't help my voice sounding thrilled. Rescuing Alban from Pilot Island, sneaking away in the fog right under their long, snooty noses. That'll show those control freaks. 'If they catch you, will they shut you up inside the walls? Never let you out again?'

But he disappoints me by saying, ''Course not!' He sounds shocked that I suggested it. 'They're not like that. They don't stop you doing things. I just don't want them to worry, that's all.'

We've reached the place where we have to split up—I go to the warden's house and he goes back behind the walls.

'See you tomorrow,' he says and smiles at me.

It makes me quivery inside, his smile. That's a nasty surprise. I'll have to be real tough with myself. 'Come on, Rachel!' I tell myself, *really* sternly, as he walks away along the beach. 'You can't be interested in him. He's so uncool. Your friends will think he's a joke.'

They'd better not. But some of them are bitches. If one of them dares say anything, I mean *anything* . . .

'Hey, Rach!' That's Stevie, calling out to me. He's down there, wandering along the beach. I know where he's been. He's been with Red Fish and his other little mates. He's trailing a piece of driftwood in the sand making a long, straight line.

'Hey, Stevie.'

He's wearing strings of skyberries round his neck, like the island children do. He's even got some round his wrists, like friendship bands. His lips are bright electric blue—like theirs. His hair's growing longer—like theirs. He doesn't look like our Stevie any more. He's like a stranger.

'Hey, Rach,' Stevie says to me again, waving.

His trainers are slopping off his feet because his shoe-laces are undone. But I don't rush to tie them for him. There's something in his eyes that stops me. Something that warns me off.

I don't know how to talk to this new Stevie. It's as if he's made a big space between us. What's he done that for? We used to be really close. He used to depend on me for everything.

At last I think of something to talk to him about. 'I borrowed your headphones, Stevie. Is that OK? I couldn't find mine. I would've asked you before but you'd gone out. And anyway, you never use your Walkman now, do you? But, here, have them back.'

Before, I wouldn't even have asked him. His room was always in such a mess that he never noticed if I borrowed stuff. But he's bound to notice now. When I took the headphones it made a hole in his nice parallel pattern. He'd probably know they were missing soon as he walked in the door.

50

But there's another reason I'm asking if it's OK. I can't explain it exactly. But it's got to do with Stevie being different now. As if he's got the right to be asked, same as anyone else.

So I take the headphones off and ram them up against his ear. 'Listen! It's that song we like.' Stevie always likes the same music I do. At least we've still got something in common.

But this time he doesn't smile and sing along. 'Have the batteries run out—?' I start asking.

Instead, he jerks his head away as if I've burnt him.

'Take them away!'

'Stevie, what's the matter?'

The music wasn't loud. It was really quiet. But he's rubbing his head, as if it hurts him. Just like Alban did.

'You can have those things,' he growls at me, pointing a shaky finger at the headphones. 'I don't want them. They're bad things. We don't need things like that on Pilot Island.'

He goes stumbling off. Leaving me staring at the headphones in my hand.

6

'What are you reading, Mum?'

I'm not really interested. But in half an hour I'm meeting Alban. And we're going to the mainland like we planned. I'm excited about it. So excited that I want to talk—about anything. Just to make the time pass quickly.

There's only Mum and me in the kitchen. Dad's outside, probably rabbit watching.

The other day he saw them do a strange thing. He went out at night and all the rabbits were out of their burrows. They were all facing north, rows and rows of them. Just sitting very still in the moonlight, facing north. 'It was spooky, Rach,' he said. 'I've never seen anything like it. Rows and rows of them.'

They bother him a lot, those rabbits. His eyes look even more far-away than usual—as if he's got serious problems to solve inside his head.

Stevie's out there too, with Red Fish and the others. Mum and Dad don't even mind if he goes out in the fog. That's how much things have changed. Before they wouldn't trust him to cross the street.

I asked Mum once: 'Aren't you worried about Stevie getting lost in the fog?'

She frowned a bit, as if she was as puzzled as I was. Then she said, 'Well, I was at first. But he doesn't ever get lost, like he used to, does he? He's never lost on Pilot Island.'

Mum finishes reading and snaps her book shut and shows me the title. It's *Sea and River Pilots of the East Coast*.

Yawn. Don't know what to say about that. Except, 'Oh, yeah. Right.'

Our kitchen window looks out towards the sea. The tide's out and the estuary is just miles of grey mud with a long line of poles vanishing into the distance. That's where me and Alban will soon be walking—beside those poles.

The morning fog is pouring out of the dunes. Soon it'll cover the whole island. Then no one will see us when we cross to the mainland.

I haven't told Mum we're going. I'm keeping it a secret. Alban is keeping it a secret too, from his mum and dad. It's stupid, isn't it? It's not like we're doing anything *criminal*. It's not like it's a *big deal*, going to the mainland for a few hours. I'm allowed to go to the mainland any time I like. And Alban wasn't worried about getting caught. But somehow it feels like a big deal. It feels dangerous. Like we're not just leaving Pilot Island—we're escaping.

Mum's face is full of questions. She's getting suspicious. She's probably wondering why I'm fidgeting and looking out the window. And why I've got my best white jeans and some make-up on. So, to put her off the scent, I get in a question of my own first.

'Why you reading about sea and river pilots?'

It works of course. My mum wants to talk. She always talks a lot when she's nervous and she's getting more and more nervous about school starting. She wants the Pilot Island children to like her, to accept her, the way they've accepted Stevie.

'I'm trying to find out a bit more about the history of Pilot Island,' Mum says. 'You know, so I can share it with the children. This old book's quite useful. I found it in Lincoln, in a second-hand book shop.'

She opens the book. There's a black and white drawing on the page. It looks just like the *Dove*, Asa Lodesman's boat.

'What kind of boat is that?'

She looks surprised that I'm asking. Like I said before, boats, even tiny ones, make me seasick.

'It's a pilot boat,' she says. 'This was a really busy estuary once. Big merchant ships came in here. From all over the world.'

I can't help showing off. 'From the Baltic ports,' I tell her, 'and from Japan.'

'How did you know that?'

I just shrug, modestly.

'Anyway, Pilot Island was famous for its brilliant pilots. They could navigate in any weather. There's an interesting little bit in this book. It says they were so good that mainlanders were scared of them. Because no pilot then could guide a ship in the dark or in fog. I mean there was no radar or anything like that. But the Pilot Islanders could do it. So the mainlanders said it was the devil's gift. They wouldn't come near Pilot Island. They said the islanders were in league with the devil.' Mum shakes her head and tuts, 'Tsk, tsk. Just silly superstition.'

I shake my head and go, 'Tsk, tsk,' too. Just to make it look like I'm paying attention.

But fog is twisting past the window. Twenty minutes to go before I meet Alban. Hope he doesn't turn up in that awful orange jumper. Hope he's scrubbed his blue skyberry lips.

Eighteen minutes to go before I meet him.

Mum's got up from the table. She's heating up some water on the camping stove. She never grumbles about being without electricity. She says, 'If the islanders can live without it, so can we.'

54

Without even thinking, I flick over the pages of her book. And there he is, staring out at me—Asa Lodesman with his stern face and beard like a snake's tongue. It's the same photo I saw yesterday on Mistress Lodesman's wall.

'What's *he* doing here?' I ask Mum.

She comes over, drying her hands: 'Who? What's who doing where?'

I jerk my thumb at the picture.

'Oh, him. He's got a great beard, hasn't he? Like Father Christmas. Wait a minute.' Mum checks the page, to see what it says. 'He started all the trouble here. It was because of him the riots started.'

'Riots?' It sounds so unlikely I have to say it again. 'Riots?'

Riots and Pilot Islanders just don't mix. Like having hot chilli sauce on your strawberry ice-cream cone. Pilot Islanders are peaceable people. Everyone knows that.

Mum sees me looking pop-eyed so she says, 'No, no, the islanders didn't riot. It was ages ago, in 1855. This man with the Father Christmas beard, he was Asa Lodesman—the best pilot on the island. A sort of local hero. Then one day, a pleasure launch needed guiding into the estuary. Look, here's a photo of her.'

Outside the fog is like a thick white wall. It's pressing against our kitchen window. Fifteen minutes until I meet Alban. So I've got time to take a quick look at the photo.

The pleasure launch in the photo is a pretty boat. She's got a sort of tent thing over the deck, like the stripy roofs you see on market stalls.

There's some writing underneath the picture.

'The *Mary Ellen*,' it says, 'was an innovative pleasure craft. She belonged to the wealthy industrialist and philanthropist Mr William Wheatstone and was named after his baby daughter, Mary Ellen Wheatstone. The *Mary Ellen* was luxurious, having brass fittings, cane seats and a canopy. But she was also the first craft of her type to be fitted with an electric motor. Electricity, it must be remembered, was at that time still a relatively new and untried invention.

'Sadly, the *Mary Ellen* came to a tragic end in June 1855 on her maiden voyage. She was lost off Wreckers' Point on Pilot Island. Nearly all on board perished, either drowned or dashed to death on the rocks. Some of the bodies were washed up days later several miles along the coast. Picnic hampers from the wreck were found as much as fifty miles away. The dead were: William Wheatstone, his wife, his baby daughter Mary Ellen, and his two young sons. Also four other ladies and gentlemen who had been invited to share their pleasure cruise and picnic.

'Only pilot Asa Lodesman survived and one family friend of the Wheatstones' who later gave evidence against him.

'Asa Lodesman was deemed to be totally responsible for the tragedy which took place in perfect weather conditions. The Wheatstones were a popular and much-loved mainland family and there was a great public outcry against Lodesman and all the Pilot Islanders who were thought to be protecting him.

'Asa Lodesman was disgraced and immediately stripped of his pilot's licence for being drunk while piloting a vessel. Many mainlanders wanted him charged with murder and taken away in chains. In the event he was charged with manslaughter. But he himself died before he could be tried for his crime at Lincoln Assizes.'

Well, well, well, I'm thinking when I get to the end of this story. Mistress Lodesman never told me all this other stuff—about her great-great-grandad getting drunk and smashing a pleasure boat on Wreckers' Point and wiping out all those people. Three children got drowned and one of them, Mary Ellen, was just a little baby. No wonder Mistress Lodesman kept quiet about *that*. How could she be so proud of him? Hanging his pilot's uniform on the wall for everyone to see? Keeping his photo and his brass telescope like he was some kind of *hero*? When he was really a murderer!

You'd think she'd want to hide all his things away and never talk about him.

'It was an excuse really.'

'What?' I was lost in my own thoughts. 'What did you say?'

'I said it was an excuse really, that shipwreck. For what the mainlanders did afterwards. It tells you all about it just over the page.'

'Tell me then—I can't be bothered to read it.'

'Well, it says the mainlanders had never liked the Pilot Islanders. Always been suspicious of them. Even scared of them. After the wreck there were big protests on the mainland. They wanted all the islanders punished, not just Asa Lodesman. One night at low tide this angry mob poured across the estuary, carrying torches. They attacked some houses, burnt them down. Two islanders got hurt. After that the islanders cut themselves off from other people. They built those high walls round themselves. Soon, they stopped going to the mainland altogether. And the book says their reputation as pilots was ruined. No ship's master ever used a pilot from this island again.'

I've got pictures in my head. Of the estuary at night. It's wide and empty and pitch black. But suddenly, there are torches blazing across it. They're coming from the mainland and moving, with deadly swiftness, towards Pilot Island.

'Good little book, isn't it?' Mum's saying. 'It tells you a lot about local history. And I almost didn't buy it.'

But, all of a sudden, local history is the last thing on my mind. Because I've just seen Alban out there in the fog. He's hanging about near the kitchen window, waiting for me. He looks like a fuzzy grey ghost but I know it's him. He actually showed up. I didn't say so before—but I was half-expecting him not to.

'Er, got to go out, Mum.'

'Not until the fog clears you're not.'

'But Stevie's allowed!'

It shows how things are topsy-turvy on Pilot Island.

Before, on the mainland, it was Stevie who wasn't allowed. He wasn't allowed to do all sorts of things. Now he's got more freedom than me! Three weeks ago, if you'd told me things would turn out like this, I'd have said, 'You must be joking.'

Mum's not going to let me go. I'll have to use a bit of psychology here. And I don't even have to lie. 'I'm just going to meet one of the island kids,' I tell her. 'I'll be all right with them. And anyway, the fog is going to clear soon.'

'Really?' Her face lights up. 'You've made a little island friend, have you?'

She's pleased. I knew she would be. She was worried before about me being on my own. That makes a change, doesn't it? Mum worrying about me instead of about Stevie? I told you things were topsy-turvy on Pilot Island.

'See you later. I might not be back until teatime.'

Mum looks even more pleased about that. I know what she's thinking. She's thinking my little island friend might be taking me home, behind the wall. She doesn't know that I'm taking *him* to the mainland.

'Hello,' says Alban, when I find him, in the fog.

He seems nervous. I keep forgetting that going to the mainland is a Big Adventure for him. Like going to a foreign country.

But he must know something about the mainland. Because he's made some changes. As if he knows what'll get him stared at. He's wearing a baggy denim shirt today instead of that cheesy jumper. And he's scrubbed the skyberry blue off his lips. They're still pale blue. But that's OK. He just looks as if he's a bit cold.

He looks all right actually. Not different at all. You'd never know he came from Pilot Island. He looks just like a mainland boy. I might not have to hide him away from my friends after all.

'We'll go to Lincoln,' I tell him, as if I haven't just decided.

'Lincoln? That's a long way away, isn't it?'

'We'll get the bus from the main road . . . And don't worry,' I tell him, grinning, 'you won't have to listen to no more mainland music. I haven't brought my stereo today.'

'What music?'

'You know, yesterday, when it made your head ache? When it messed up your brain?'

I'm still grinning but he looks sort of blank, as if he doesn't remember. He's probably just too nervous. He says, 'Will I need money on the mainland? I haven't got any money.'

'I have.' And I rustle the notes I've got in my pocket. 'The buses go every half an hour. So even if we just miss one, we won't have long to wait.'

It feels great to be going to the mainland. I know my way around there. I know how things work. On Pilot Island there are so many things I don't understand.

'Come on, Alban. Let's go.'

But there's fog all around us. It's not so thick now. It's going to break up soon. But it's squirming about like worms. It plays tricks with your senses. I don't know which direction I'm facing. Are the sand dunes in front of me? Or is it the open estuary? I can't even work out where our house is. I'm a few minutes walk from my own back door. But I'm totally lost and confused.

I have to ask Alban: 'Which way is the mainland?' I hate being lost and helpless. But, somehow, Pilot Island makes me feel like that.

Alban doesn't hesitate. He just answers, 'This way, of course,' and dives right into the fog.

I'm panicking—thinking, He's forgotten I can't home! —when he pops up again.

'Keep close behind me,' he says. And dives back into the fog.

There's nothing to do but keep close, like he said. I'm so close I bet he can feel my breath on his neck.

But all the time I'm thinking, Wait until we get to the mainland. That's *my* neighbourhood. That's where I know the way. Let's see who's helpless then.

7

We're somewhere out in the estuary, deep in fog. I'm keeping very close to Alban—I keep treading on the back of his scruffy trainers. 'Whoops, sorry.'

I've been having these nightmares. About getting lost in the fog and ending up neck-deep in swirling, salty water. And in these nightmares I always cry out, 'Help, help!' and I know the islanders are in the fog with me, listening to me drown. But not one of them comes to save me.

I hate the fog. Wonder if Alban *really* knows where the mainland is? I can't see the poles. Or the tree-house on stilts where you climb to escape from the sea. If Alban ran off now and left me here, I'd be helpless.

To take my mind off it I try making some conversation. Talking as we walk. Only, my voice doesn't sound casual like I want it to. It sounds small and scared.

'My mum's got this old book. Whoops, sorry.' I've stepped on his shoes again. 'It's called *Sea and River Pilots of the East Coast*. Dead boring title, isn't it? But there's a bit in it about Asa Lodesman. You know, Mistress Lodesman acted like he was some kind of hero and a brilliant pilot and everything? Well, in this book, the one my mum's got, it says he got drunk and wrecked this boat the *Mary Ellen* and a whole family called the Wheatstones and their friends got drowned. And everyone called him a murderer. And some mainlanders came over and attacked the islanders. They had these torches . . .'

I can't seem to get that bit out of my head, those blazing torches. And it's stupid but the other bit I keep seeing is those picnic hampers from the *Mary Ellen*. All smashed to bits and washed up on some lonely beach miles and miles away.

'Doesn't she know about what it says in the book? About her great-great-grandad being a murderer? Doesn't she know that story?'

Alban suddenly turns round in the fog. It startles me because his seawater green eyes are really close to mine.

I think for a second he's going to get really mad and say something like, 'How dare you say that about Asa Lodesman, we all think he's great!' But he doesn't say that. He just shrugs and says, ''Course she knows the story. We all know the story of Asa Lodesman. She just doesn't believe it, that's all.'

'But it's in a book. It must be true. I'll bring it to show you, if you like. There's a photo of him and everything.'

'It is true. Everything you just said happened. But she doesn't believe it was his fault. She says he would never get drunk when he was piloting a ship.'

'But this book says a man got saved from the wreck. And he was a witness. He said that Asa Lodesman was drunk. So how can she say that it wasn't his fault? She wasn't there. She wasn't even born yet—it was ages ago, over a hundred years.'

'I know,' Alban says. 'The story says he was staggering about, couldn't even speak properly. But Mistress Lodesman says a great injustice was done. She says he shouldn't have lost his pilot's licence. Or his good name.'

'So what does she say happened then?'

Alban sighs. He's not looking at me now. He's staring away through the fog. He's thinking about the mainland, not about Asa Lodesman.

'She should forget about it,' he says. 'Nobody else even thinks about it. We're not famous pilots any more. We're fishermen now.'

He starts walking again and I've got to follow him. But there's one more thing I want to know.

'How did he die?'

'Who? Asa Lodesman?'

'Yes. Mum's book says he died before they could try him for manslaughter.'

'He drowned. He left his pilot uniform behind and his boat and his telescope and he just walked out into the fog and he drowned.'

'How did he get lost in the fog? He could home, couldn't he?'

' 'Course he could home—he was a brilliant navigator. He didn't get lost. He killed himself. Just waited for the sea to come in and let it drown him. Because he couldn't bear the disgrace.'

'Oh. Right.'

Those creepy thoughts are crowding in. I can't stop them. I can see the sea closing over Asa Lodesman's head. Like it closed over the head of the last warden. Like it nearly closed over mine. Only, Asa Lodesman didn't even struggle or shout. He just stood there and waited for it to drown him. How could he do that?

And I'm still thinking about it when, suddenly, like magic, the fog lifts.

And there's sunshine and blue sky and the whole estuary's so dazzling it nearly blinds you. Way behind us the white beaches of Pilot Island sparkle. Something flashes out from Wreckers' Point like a diamond. What *is* that? I try to picture Wreckers' Point in my mind—Mistress Lodesman's cottage, the lighthouse, the *Dove* down on the beach. Nothing sparkly there. Unless it's the cottage windows. It flashes again. Then it's gone. So I stop looking back at Pilot Island and turn round.

'We're here,' says Alban.

And there's the last pole, right in front of us. All we've got to do is walk up the beach and we're on the mainland.

'Good guess! We're in exactly the right place.'

I'm trying to congratulate him but he just shrugs as if it's a stupid thing to say.

'I didn't guess,' he tells me. 'Homing's got nothing to do with guessing.'

For a second I feel like giving him a good slap because he sounds so superior. They're all like that on Pilot Island. Think they're better than anyone else. No wonder those mainlanders back in 1855 wanted to teach them a lesson.

But I can't stay mad for long because Alban's so thrilled at being on the mainland. He's like a little kid.

'I've walked up this road a bit,' he tells me like he's confessing to something really wild. 'Once, when Dad brought his boat over to unload some fish. But then it was time to go and he called me back.'

'And you didn't feel ill or anything?'

'No, I felt quite fine.'

'See! I told you they'd invented that, about the mainland making you ill. They just invented it to keep you on Pilot Island. I mean, they had to invent something didn't they? Because it's so *boring* on Pilot Island that all the young people would just clear off to the mainland and never come back. And anyway, what about your Go-Between? Mistress Lodesman doesn't get sick does she? And she's always nipping over here. I've seen her . . . '

I've got to pause for breath but I must have convinced him because he starts striding out along the road. Actually it's not a road, it's a dirt track. He just thinks it's a road. We don't hit a real road for a couple of miles yet. And that's where we're going to wait for the bus. I've got it all planned out.

'Wait for me!' I run after him and shove past him. We're on the mainland. On my home ground. So I'm the leader now.

'That's a cow over there,' I tell him in my mum's teacher voice. 'And those great big metal towers that we're coming to are pylons that carry electricity. And that's a big red combine harvester over there in that field.'

'Look,' Alban grins at me, 'I've never been to the mainland. But I know the names of things. I know how things work. I've read books. I've read magazines and newspapers that Mistress Lodesman brings home.'

'Oh, sorry, I'm sure.' I can't help sounding a bit huffy. I was looking forward to teaching him things, to answering his questions. I thought he'd be as clueless on the mainland as I am on Pilot Island.

Then he surprises me by asking, 'Is this kind of shirt all right to wear on the mainland? I don't want the mainlanders to laugh at me.'

I didn't think Pilot Islanders cared what mainlanders thought about them. But he looks so worried that I give him my biggest, most reassuring smile. 'Nobody will laugh at you,' I tell him. 'They'd better not. You're with me, aren't you? And anyway, you look great. You look just like a mainlander.'

And he smiles back like I've just paid him a massive compliment.

We walk a few steps and he starts to ask something else. But he only gets as far as, 'What—?' when suddenly he drops to his knees, like he's been smashed on the back of the head with a baseball bat.

He tries to get up and walk. But he goes lurching round in circles like he's drunk. He's trying to say something. It might be my name but it just comes out all slurred, 'Rurrr, Rurrr.'

65

'What's the matter? Alban? Hey, what's the matter?' I don't know what to do—I try to take his arm but he pushes me away. 'I'm going to be surr-surr-sick.'

Then, I can't believe what he does next. I can feel my eyes stretching wide with the shock. He grabs his head in both hands as if his skull is going to explode and starts beating it on the dirt track, *bam, bam, bam*!

'Stop it, you'll hurt yourself.'

I try to pull him up but it's like he's in a fit or something. His forehead is stuck with sharp gravel. There's blood trickling down his face. But now his eyes are rolling up and he's moaning!

Then he just collapses, curls up on the ground like a baby. But his legs are still kicking, kicking. There's foamy spit coming out of his mouth.

I can't think—it's a nightmare. My mind's useless. It's just twittering at me like a caveful of bats. I kneel down beside him.

'Alban!'

He doesn't seem to see me or hear me. He's trying to push himself up on his hands and knees. He crawls in a circle like a sick animal. Then his arms and legs start to wobble like he can't control them. And he falls over sideways, crunch, on to the track.

I'm really panicking now. I stare all around. No people. No help anywhere.

Then I hear it. The slap, slap, slap of sandals hurrying down the track. I've never been so glad to see anyone in my life. Even though it's Mistress Lodesman, the Go-Between.

She's got Asa Lodesman's brass telescope in her hand.

She pushes it at me and says, 'Hold this.' It's heavy, heavier than I thought. Then she ignores me, grabs Alban under the armpits and starts heaving him back down the track, towards the beach. He's stopped twitching and moaning. And he's just flopping, with his head hanging back.

It's like Mistress Lodesman has got the strength of Superwoman. She's panting hard but she's really tough. Her blue hair was pinned up in a bun. It comes tumbling down all over her face but she doesn't stop.

I should help. I should help to carry him because his feet are trailing. They're digging scrape marks in the dirt. I run after them and try to pick up Alban's legs. But she shoots me a really dangerous look through her hair. It scares me. She looks like a wicked witch. So I back off and let her drag him on her own.

She hauls him back to the beach and lays him gently on the sand. He just sprawls out, not moving.

Mistress Lodesman straightens up, sort of clutching at her chest. For a minute she closes her eyes and sways and I think, 'She's going to get sick too!' But she doesn't. She does some deep breathing. And when she opens her eyes again, they're cold as green ice and they're staring straight into mine. Like she's waiting for me to apologize or something.

'What's . . . what's wrong with him?'

My eyes flick away from her to look at Alban again. He looks peaceful now, resting in the white sand with seashells all around him. Too peaceful. My hands are trembling, I can't stop them so I jam them deep in my pockets. But that's not much good because my voice is trembling too. 'He . . . he's not dead, is he?'

Mistress Lodesman gives a snort. 'Dead? No, he's not dead. Can't you see he's breathing?'

'Well, what's wrong with him then? You should have seen him back there. He was going crazy. He was—'

'The mainland is wrong with him,' she interrupts me.

67

Her voice is chilly as her eyes. 'Didn't you know the mainland is bad for island people? That it makes them ill? It was lucky for you that I happened to be looking out over the estuary with Grandfather Lodesman's telescope. I saw you when the fog lifted. And I came after you. By the way, I'll have the telescope back now.'

I hand it over without saying anything.

My throat feels like it's packed with pebbles. I keep trying to gulp them down but they won't go. She scares me. It's like she thinks I'm responsible. I didn't ask him to come, did I. Did I? I can't remember now whose idea it was.

Then someone says, 'It's not her fault, Mistress Lodesman. I asked her to come. I wanted to see the mainland.'

Alban's sitting up. He's white and shaky but he seems OK. Except he looks very confused.

'What happened to me?' he says. 'I remember . . . I remember a buzzing in my head, then being dizzy and my head spinning round, then this pain . . . '

Mistress Lodesman shakes her head, sighing. I thought she'd be mad with him because she's such an old dragon. But when she speaks her voice is gentle not fierce. And, maybe my ears are playing tricks, but she sounds sad too. Very sad.

'You're not the first,' she says to Alban. 'Some are content to live their whole lives on Pilot Island. They never feel restless for the mainland. They believe what they are told—that islanders cannot tolerate the mainland. That they are allergic to it and it makes them ill even to visit it. But some, like you, are curious. They must try things for themselves.'

'I just wanted to see . . . !' Alban's struggling to get up.

'Shhh! Shhh!' says the Go-Between, softly. 'I do not blame you. I was like you once. I crossed the estuary one day. I wanted to see for myself too.'

'But it didn't make you ill, did it? Not like it made me just now?'

'No. I'm different to the other islanders. I can't explain why.'

There's a thought itching in my brain. I wonder why Mistress Lodesman came back to Pilot Island? Once she found out she wasn't allergic to the mainland, why didn't she just think, Great! I'm out of here! and keep on walking? That's what I would have done. I wouldn't come back to make their skyberry wine and teach their freaky kids and be their Go-Between. I'd keep right on walking and never look back.

They're talking together now, Mistress Lodesman and Alban. Whispering secrets with their heads close together like I'm not there.

Then she helps him up. 'The sickness will pass very quickly,' she tells Alban. 'Let's go home. The further you get from the mainland the better you will feel.'

Pilot Island is sparkling in the sun like it's made of silver. Both of them shade their eyes and take a long, long look at it. I know what they're thinking. They're wishing they were already back there.

They start walking, alongside the poles. At first Alban walks slowly, leaning on her like a very old man who's scared he might fall down again. Then he gets quicker and shakes off her arm and starts striding out across the estuary. Neither of them look back. They don't seem to care if I'm following them or not.

That's it then. All my plans are ruined. And my white jeans are dirty. I was going to take him to the pictures this afternoon and buy popcorn and sit in the back row.

Suppose I could still go to Lincoln by myself. Maybe Sophie will go to the pictures with me.

But I don't feel like it now. I just can't be bothered. There's only one place to go really.

So I follow them back across the estuary towards Pilot Island.

I'm at the tree-house now. I mean, the refuge. I've never been this close to it before. The legs look like they're made of seaweed and barnacles. But I give one of them a kick, *clang*. They're made of iron. I'm just looking up the ladder thinking, It's a long climb up there, when *Rrrrrr*, I hear an engine.

Something green shoots out of the wobbly heat haze. It zooms towards me, like it's flying across the sands. It's Dad's jeep. It stops right beside me.

'Get in,' Dad says. 'Would you like a trip to the mainland?'

Mum and Stevie are in the jeep. Mum says, 'I thought you were meeting your friend.' I just mumble something and climb in the back with Stevie.

He looks fed up. He's sitting all slumped up and he won't even look at me. So I poke him. 'What's wrong with you?' He just growls 'Grrrr.' I thought he'd got over having moods. He'd better not start anything with me. I'm not in a very good mood myself.

Mum laughs. 'Oh, take no notice—we're a bit grumpy, aren't we, Stevie? I told him he has to have some new shoes and get his hair cut. But he didn't want to come. He says he never wants to go away from Pilot Island. He says he wants to stay here forever.'

And Dad and Mum laugh like it's a joke. They don't see anything to worry about.

But I don't think it's a joke. I take another look at Stevie. His lips aren't skyberry blue. They're red, like they've been scrubbed. And he isn't wearing his skyberry friendship bands. He's got shoes on—he's been going round with bare feet lately, like the island kids do. He's got a clean, ironed shirt on and a crisp pair of blue jeans. And he looks really, really miserable.

Mum twists her head round and sees me inspecting Stevie. She laughs. 'I had to clean him up for the mainland. He didn't like it at all, did you, Stevie? Dad practically had to hold him down while I scrubbed his face. What a fuss. You'd think I was going to kill him!'

Stevie glares at her behind her back like he wants to kill *her*.

'You talk to him,' says Mum. 'See if you can get him in a good mood. Tell him we'll only be away from his precious Pilot Island for a couple of hours.'

What's the use of me telling him anything? Stevie and me are like strangers these days. He doesn't listen to me any more. I can't understand why Mum hasn't noticed that.

Dad's quiet as usual, like he's concentrating on driving. But I bet he isn't. I bet he's got rabbits on the brain. Bet his brain is hopping with them.

'Hey, Dad, found any more bunnies that dig their burrows from north to south? Did you ever think that maybe they've got compasses down there with them? Maybe they do geography at rabbit school. Maybe they've all got these teeny weeny rabbit compasses inside their burrows. You have a look next time and I bet you'll find one.'

I know—it's a feeble thing to say. But I'm only trying to be cheerful. Trying to take my mind off Alban and what just happened. But nobody wants to be cheerful with me.

We're driving past the last pole now. There's the dirt track. You can see the scrape-marks of Alban's shoes. I

71

don't want to think about that—it's too scary. So instead I feel in my pocket, to make sure my money's safe. I'm going to buy myself make-up, magazines, clothes, loads of things. I might buy a new CD. Ready for when our wind turbine comes, on Monday.

The jeep's bumping along the track. We're at the place where Alban collapsed. There are the pylons and the red combine harvester in the field.

'Ooooooooooow!'

I nearly jump out of my skin. There's a terrible howling noise right next to my ear. It's Stevie. He's staring round and his eyes are wild. He's holding his head like it really hurts him.

Then he starts banging his head on the back of Mum's seat.

'Stevie!' Mum's shouting. Her face is white with shock. She can't believe it. 'Don't do that. I thought you'd stopped doing that. I thought you'd stopped making scenes.'

'He isn't making a scene. His head hurts. Back the jeep up. Back the jeep up NOW!'

I'm not usually so sure about things. But I know, for an absolute certainty, that we've got to get Stevie away from the mainland and back to Pilot Island.

'Don't be silly,' says Mum. 'He needs his hair cut. We're not going all the way back just because he's started this silly head-banging behaviour again.'

There's spit coming out of Stevie's mouth.

He's making a terrible, high-pitched whining sound. He's frantic to get out of the jeep, scrabbling at the doors.

'He wants to be sick,' I tell Mum.

I'm trying to help him but he's flinging his arms about. He whacks me right in the mouth.

'Ow!'

72

'Stevie!' says Mum. 'Apologize to Rachel immediately!' She was shocked and angry before. Now she sounds scared.

Stevie doesn't apologize. He can't even hear what she's saying. He doesn't know where he is, what he's doing.

I wipe the blood off my lips. For a second I feel like hitting him back, even though I know he didn't do it deliberately.

'He's made her mouth bleed!' Mum's telling Dad.

Dad's stopped the car. 'What on earth's going on back there?' he says, like he's only just noticed.

He turns around. Stevie's writhing around, trying to smash his skull on the seats. But he can't because they're not hard enough.

'Stevie, for God's sake!'

'Dad, listen to me. Are you listening? You have to take Stevie back to Pilot Island. He's not making a scene. Honest. He can't help it. This is what happened to Alban. I saw it, just half an hour ago. This is what happens to them when they come to the mainland. Now it's happening to Stevie. The Go-Between saved Alban by taking him back. You've got to take Stevie back too.'

Dad doesn't understand. You can tell by the bewildered look on his face. But he *was* listening. Because he takes another look at Stevie and slams the jeep into reverse. Looking over his shoulder he goes speeding down the track, and on to the beach. He doesn't stop until we're way out in the estuary.

Then he switches off the engine.

Stevie's stopped howling and moaning. We just sit there—in the jeep in dead silence in the middle of the estuary. We seem to sit there, not saying anything, for ages, just staring out at all that sunshine dazzle. All those miles of sand and sea and blue, blue sky.

Dad speaks first. He says, without turning round, 'Is Stevie all right?'

Stevie answers for himself. He looks really pale but he's calm again. 'I want to go back home now,' he says. Then he points a shaky finger at Mum. 'And don't *you* make me go to the mainland *ever* again.'

Mum doesn't say anything. It's like she's too stunned to speak.

But I'm sure Dad knows something. I've thought that for days now. That he's discovered some of Pilot Island's secrets.

But if he knows them, he doesn't tell us. He starts the engine and turns the jeep around so we're heading towards Pilot Island. There's Wreckers' Point. It's round the other side of the island but you can just see it, curving out into the estuary. You can't see Mistress Lodesman's cottage or the *Dove*. But you can see the burnt-out lighthouse, like a wart on the end of a grey finger.

We're driving back now. Still, no one says anything. I wonder where Mistress Lodesman took Alban. I wonder if he's sitting in her cottage now, in that weird blue glow of skyberry wine bottles. Maybe he's gone back to his mum and dad, behind those high walls. Wherever he is, I feel like he's been taken away from me, just when I thought we were getting close.

We're back at the warden's cottage. Stevie says, 'I'm going to see my friends.' And he just climbs out of the jeep. Mum doesn't even try to stop him.

He rips some skyberries off a bush, tilts his head back and throws them one by one into his mouth. He crunches them until blue juice trickles down his chin. Then, he breaks into this sort of clumsy shuffle. That's Stevie running, he always runs like that. Anyway, he shuffles up to the top of a dune. At the top he turns round and scowls and shows us his fist. Then straightaway he changes the scowl to a big grin and lets his fist spring open and waggles his fingers around. He's saying something.

'What's he saying?' says Mum. 'I can't hear him.'

I can't hear him either but I know what he's saying.

'He's saying, "Bunch of flowers",' I tell her. 'It's Stevie's idea of a joke.'

He waggles his fingers some more, then gives us a cheery wave and disappears down the other side of the dunes.

'He seems quite happy now, doesn't he?' says Mum, as if she's begging for us to agree with her. 'Everything seems all right again, doesn't it?'

But I'm not going to agree with her. I don't think everything's all right. What about what happened twenty minutes ago? Twenty minutes ago Stevie was screaming and trying to smash his head to a pulp and saying, 'Don't take me to the mainland ever again!'

Dad won't answer her either. He doesn't think everything's all right. I can tell because he's gripping the driving wheel very tight, even though we've stopped. He's gripping it so hard that his knuckles are white as bones.

'Well, I think he just got himself into a little mood,' Mum's saying in a stubborn voice. 'He never did like having his hair cut. But he's happy again. So everything *must* be all right now.'

8

It's after midnight. Mum and Dad have finally gone to bed. They'd been downstairs talking for ages. I don't know what about. But when they stay up late and talk in loud, worried whispers it's usually about Stevie.

I tiptoed half-way down the stairs and tried to listen. But it was no good. The rain made too much racket on the windows. Except I think I heard my name, *Rachel* this and *Rachel* that. But that doesn't make sense. I can't have been hearing right. It's Stevie they worry about. Not me. They never worry about me.

I heard thunder growl just now. It was far off, over the mainland somewhere. But it's getting closer. Dad says there's a big storm coming.

Stevie's been OK since we brought him back from the mainland two days ago. OK that is if you think it's OK to run around in the fog with Red Fish with skyberry blue lips and bare feet and strings of skyberries hanging round your neck. And to keep your room like a neatness freak with all your stuff arranged in parallel lines.

Mum says, 'He's so happy here, so confident, he's like a new person. I don't know why but he can cope with his dyspraxia much better on Pilot Island.'

But I liked the old Stevie better. I liked him before he could cope.

I haven't seen Alban for two days now. If he's not around tomorrow I'm going out to Wreckers' Point to ask Mistress Lodesman about him. She'll probably blame me for taking him to the mainland but I don't care. I've got to know if he's all right. And if he blames me too.

There's some good news. Actually it's good news and bad news. The good news is—they came to fix our wind turbine. Yay! The bad news is—it's going to take them two more days. *Two more days* before we get electricity. Dad's really proud because our electricity's coming from wind power. 'It's so safe and environmentally friendly. Just a little windmill turning in our back yard. Nobody can object to that.'

Bam! There's a big explosion over the house. It's thunder. The storm's made a direct hit on Pilot Island.

Bam! There it goes again. My bedroom lights up with a blue flash. I pull back the curtains, look out at the estuary. Wow, there's lightning sizzling between the sky and the water. Great crooked spikes of electricity, *flash, flash, flash.* They're lighting the estuary up, bright as day.

I can see the wooden poles. And the refuge on its iron legs. It doesn't look like a tree-house now. It looks like a giant spider squatting out there in the mud.

I'm not scared. Storms have never scared me. But there's no point in trying to sleep with all that row going on.

So I go downstairs to the kitchen to get myself something to eat. *Bam, bam, bam*—it's like the house is rocking, being biffed like a punchbag. I throw back my head and laugh 'Ha, ha!' I *like* storms. I love them actually. Thunder and lightning and rain and wind all crashing and booming and banging and screaming like the best and biggest rock concert ever. You feel like you ought to applaud.

There's nobody else about. Thought Stevie would have woken up.

I bet he'll come wandering down in a minute rubbing his eyes: 'What's all that noise, Rach?'

And I'll say, 'It's all right. It's only a storm. You're safe with me here.'

Except I forgot, Stevie doesn't need me to make him feel safe any more.

I can't light that stinky old oil lamp—it scorches my eyebrows every time. So I light a candle instead. Then I sit at the kitchen table crunching cornflakes watching the shadows chasing each other all over the walls, listening to the storm getting wilder and wilder outside.

Mum's book is on the table—*Sea and River Pilots of the East Coast*. Just for something to do I flick through the pages. Nothing interesting, and I'm tired, I can't stop yawning.

I'm thinking, Time for bed, Rach.

Then my eye catches something, some words written under a photo. 'Wreckers' Point,' it says.

I pull the candle closer so me and the book are together in a little circle of light.

There's a black and white photograph of a lighthouse.

'The Wreckers' Point lighthouse,' it says. 'This electrically powered lighthouse was constructed on Pilot Island in 1876. It sent out a white/red alternating flash every thirty seconds visible for seventeen miles in clear weather.'

It must be the lighthouse that burnt down. It doesn't say anything here about it burning down. As I turn the page my hand is trembling, I don't know why. There's some more writing about the lighthouse on Wreckers' Point.

'It was assumed,' Mum's book says, 'that the danger of fire would be much less in an electrically lighted house than in one using coal or oil. But on the very night it started operating, the lighthouse on Wreckers' Point was destroyed by fire.'

The book tells you some other stuff. How the heat inside the lighthouse was so great that the granite blocks it was built from glowed fiery red. How from the mainland the burning lighthouse looked like a crimson tower and the sea around it was crimson too, as if it was made of blood.

And at the bottom of the page it says, 'A swift boat was dispatched from the mainland to try and save the lighthouse. But the mainlanders were driven from the building by red-hot iron bolts and falling beams and molten lead pouring from the roof.

'Nothing is known of the cause of the fire for the engineer from the mainland, who tended the electric light, was never found. It was thought that, in his panic at the great conflagration and furnace-like heat, he leapt off from Wreckers' Point and was drowned in the treacherous estuary tides.

'No other lighthouse was ever built on Pilot Island. Soon after this date the river began to silt up. Despite desperate attempts to dredge it, it became impassable to ocean-going vessels. The busy ports along it fell into a decline. The estuary lost its importance as a centre of commerce and became the remote and forgotten backwater it is today.'

'Remote and forgotten backwater' is dead right. That just describes the estuary and Pilot Island. Like I said before, the bumhole of the world.

The candle's started smoking so I blow it out and now I'm completely in the dark.

That mainlander—the engineer who looked after the light. It said, 'Drowned in the treacherous estuary tides.' Just thinking about it makes me icy cold. Bet it was foggy too. Just like it was when the last warden's house burned down and she ran off in a panic.

I'm just thinking about how weird that is—two mysterious fires, two mainlanders drowned—when *Blam!* a crash of thunder almost splits the walls. The kitchen turns a spooky blue from a lightning flash and I have to rush to the window to check what's going on. Why hasn't Stevie woken up?

Soon as I pull back the curtain I know why he hasn't woken up. Because he's already awake. He's out there, in the stormy night. The lightning just flashed again and I saw him really clearly like in a bright white spotlight—his skyberry lips and his spiky brown hair. I saw all the islanders. They're out there too—down on the beach. What's going on?

'Calm down, Rach, they're probably collecting sea coal.'

That's what I try to tell myself, at first. Because they do that sometimes—I've seen them. When the tide brings sea coal in they all rush out to collect it for their fires.

But then the beach lights up, *flash*, and there's no black sea coal there. Not a single bit. The beach is white as a snowdrift.

So what're they doing?

When you see them, they're always busy. Always going somewhere—to their fishing boats or the oyster beds. Always calm and peaceful and minding their own business. But now they're out there in a big mob. Sort of . . . just milling about. Rushing backwards and forwards like grey ghosts in the moonlight. Some of them are running round in circles. What's wrong with them? Why are they all so upset? It's dangerous out there—they'll get struck by lightning.

Zippp, zippp, the lightning crackles and the beach is lit up by brilliant silvery light. Then it goes dark again.

But I saw their faces, streaming with rain. I saw their eyes. Their eyes were wild, like cattle. You know those cowboy films where the cattle stampede and you get a close-up of their eyes all wild and scared and rolling? Well, the islanders' eyes looked like that. And their mouths were open wide like blue caves. And there was Stevie in the mob, with Red Fish. All running about, bumping into each other like a bunch of crazy dancers.

Another *zippp*.

There's Alban! He's looking this way and for a minute I think he's seen me. But his crazy cattle eyes aren't seeing anything. He runs into the blackness of the dunes and I can't see him any more. I can't pick out Stevie or Red Fish. They're just a crowd of black shapes in the dark . . .

The lightning seems to have stopped now. The thunder's still around but it's rumbling into the distance. The storm's moving away from Pilot Island. It's moving out to the open sea.

I let the curtains fall and shrink back behind them. I'm scared. I don't want them to see me spying on them. I'm a mainlander—like the last warden and the lighthouse engineer. And look what happened to them.

It's funny but I don't feel scared for Stevie. I don't even think of him as a mainlander any more. He's one of them now, an islander. And a queasy thought comes into my head. If he had to choose—between them and me—whose side would he be on?

Don't know how long I stand there in the dark, hiding behind the curtains.

Someone creeps in the back door. It's Stevie. I can see him but he can't see me. He's drenched with rain. His shoe-laces are dangling, like always.

I nearly leap out of my hiding place shouting, 'Come here, Stevie. Your shoes are undone!'

But something holds me back. I can't fix everything for him like I used to. He's changed, or I've changed. I don't know exactly. But I feel like I haven't got the right. Like he's got his own life now. And I mustn't interfere—unless he asks me to.

So I stay put near the window and watch him go upstairs to his bedroom. He's walking very slowly, *plod, plod, plod,* as if he's exhausted after all that rushing round on the beach. I can't see his eyes. But I bet they're not mad cattle eyes any more. They're probably just tired out, like the rest of him.

Before I go back to bed I peep through the curtains again to check what's going on. There's nobody out there. Not a living soul. The islanders have gone back behind their high walls. And all I'm looking at is a peaceful silver moon and a wide, empty beach.

9

I've got to see Alban. I really need to.

So I'm walking round to Wreckers' Point. He said he goes there often, to give Mistress Lodesman skyberries or driftwood or to do some work on the *Dove*.

I want to ask him this: 'What the hell was going on last night in the storm?'

But maybe I won't ask him. It depends on what he's like. He might not want to be friends, not after he got so sick on the mainland. Those islanders have probably warned him off:

'Don't have anything to do with that mainland girl. Remember, Pilot Island: good; mainland: bad.'

It's a pity because I was beginning to like him. Once you got used to those skyberry lips and those home-made clothes he was quite fanciable really.

I bet Mistress Lodesman warned him off: 'Be a good boy, Alban.'

That would be just like her. She didn't like me anyway. When we were in her cottage and she was going on about Asa Lodesman and what a hero he was, she never smiled at me once. She just looked, sort of proud and haughty.

Hero, my bottom. Wonder what she'd say if she knew I knew the truth. That her precious great-great-grandad got drunk and wrecked the *Mary Ellen* and drowned all those people? Bet she wouldn't look so haughty then.

I must stop thinking about people getting drowned. The list seems to be getting longer and longer. The people on the *Mary Ellen*, Asa Lodesman, the lighthouse engineer, the last warden. And me, when I got lost in the fog.

'You idiot, Rach, you didn't get drowned,' I tell myself, out loud.

I know, but I nearly did.

Think about something else.

It's foggy out there in the estuary even though it's almost afternoon. The fog's been hanging around all day. One minute you can see for miles. The next you can't see your hand in front of your face.

Think about something else.

I didn't see Mistress Lodesman going crazy with the others in the storm last night. Why wasn't she there? Maybe she was brewing skyberry wine. Or shining the buttons on Asa Lodesman's uniform. Maybe she was being the Go-Between and away on the mainland. Maybe she was there and I just didn't see her.

I didn't ask Stevie about the storm. He was still asleep when I left our house. I peeped round his bedroom door and he was just a lump under his duvet. His arm was dangling out of bed on to the floor. It had messed up his neat parallel lines of cars.

I thought, I bet the first thing he does when he wakes up is straighten those cars up.

Without thinking, I did something I always used to do. I looked under his duvet to see if he had his Walkman on. Stevie used to go to sleep listening to music. And the headphone wires would get tangled round his neck. So every night I'd take the headphones off in case he strangled himself in his sleep. I'd do it very gently, without waking him up. I used to do that every single night. I never forgot once.

But all that was before we came to Pilot Island. I had to remind myself, 'Rach, he doesn't need looking after any more.' And, anyway, he didn't have his headphones on. I forgot, he doesn't use his Walkman

84

now. Not since we came to Pilot Island. He says it makes him sick.

Think about something else . . .

There's Dad, over there in the dunes.

I don't have to ask him what he's doing. He's doing his favourite thing—kneeling in piles of blue bunny poo, studying rabbits. They're all around him, really tame. They're probably used to him now. They probably think he's Big Chief Rabbit.

Dad sees me and calls out, 'Rachel, come here. I think I've found the answer!'

'What?'

'I've found out why these rabbits behave like they do. Why they build their burrows north to south. Why they sit facing north. And it's amazing. Biologically it's truly amazing.'

I push through the skyberry and gorse bushes to get to where Dad is. Everywhere there are white tails flickering. It's rabbits, scooting off down their holes.

Dad's in his camouflage jacket, as usual, with the pockets bulging with stuff. He's just folding up his little computer.

He's really excited. 'It was something you said that got me thinking. That joke you made—about these rabbits having compasses in their burrows.'

Did I make a feeble joke like that? Shame on me.

But Dad's rushing on. He's dying to tell me what he's found out.

'Well, they do have compasses. But not in their burrows. The compasses are inside their heads.'

I raise my eyebrows sky-high: 'Are you kidding me?' My dad's got some funny ideas. But this is a bit wild, even for him.

'No, really, Rach. I'm not kidding. It's all to do with

the skyberries the rabbits eat. That's my theory. Skyberries are full of mineral iron—we already know that. That's probably why the migrating birds really like them.'

'I don't get it. What's iron got to do with anything?'

'See, Rach, migrating birds like pigeons have got these tiny iron particles in their brain. Didn't I tell you this before? Remember, when you did that school project on magnetism?'

I nod and look wise. But I don't remember really.

'Anyway, each one of these iron particles behaves like a little magnet; you know, like a compass needle. So these birds have got their own built-in compasses. That makes them natural navigators. They know where north and south are, instinctively. Nobody tells them. It's like a sixth sense.'

'So what does eating the skyberries do then? Top up the iron in their brain or something? Make them even better navigators?'

'Exactly!' cries Dad as if I'm a genius. 'That's exactly right. But I think the skyberries are doing it to the rabbits too. I mean giving them tiny compasses in their brains. I don't know how—these skyberries have got a really special chemistry. It needs a lot more research. It's something to do with the iron compounds being soluble, being able to bond with brain cells. But I've got to get more proof.'

'Huh! How could you prove something like that?'

'Lots of ways. I could slice up a rabbit's brain, look at it under an electron microscope and see if there's a build-up of magnetic iron in it.'

'Yuk! You wouldn't do that, would you?'

'I would if I had an electron microscope handy. This is a really big discovery, Rach. These skyberries are amazing—plants that give mammals the same instinctive sense of direction as homing pigeons. That's something incredible.'

Now, I do biology at school. And some things I don't remember. But I remember this: 'People are mammals,' I tell Dad.

'What?' he says.

'People are mammals.'

I can see his brain working away like mad. My dad isn't very interested in people. He's interested in teeny-weeny beetles that other people squash under their shoes. He's an expert on all kinds of animal behaviour. But he doesn't notice people behaviour. So I don't think he's thought about what I'm suggesting. Until this minute. But the more I think about it the more excited I get. My brain's fizzing with it. 'Look, Dad, which way is north?'

My dad points out over the estuary. 'That way is due north.'

'I knew it! That's the way Stevie's bedroom window faces. All his stuff is lined up facing his window—in parallel lines, north to south like a compass needle points! Even his bed. He even likes sleeping north to south. He says it doesn't *feel* right sleeping any other way. Can't you see, Dad, *Stevie's* behaving like he's got a compass needle in his head? Just like the rabbits and birds. And he can home can't he? He knows which direction is which, even in the fog. And all the islanders can do that, can't they? They can find their way in the dark and in fog as if they've got compasses in their heads. I didn't understand how they could do it before but I do now. They eat skyberries *all the time*. They practically live on them! And Stevie eats them all the time too, but I don't and I can't home. I nearly drowned in the fog so I haven't got a compass in *my* brain so that proves it doesn't it—?'

'Wait a minute,' Dad interrupts me. 'Hang on a minute there, Rach.'

It's all a bit jumbled but I know what I mean. I mean, if skyberries can give the rabbits compasses in their heads, then why can't they do it to the islanders? What if the islanders are compass-heads too? That would explain some of the freaky things they do—like homing.

They're just iron heads, that's all. Compass brains. And there's no big mystery about it. It doesn't make them special or clever or superhuman or anything. It's scientific, it's chemistry. I could home if I wanted to. I could be an iron head too if I drank skyberry wine and skyberry juice and wore them like jewellery and ate them like sweets.

Dad's saying, 'That's a very interesting idea, Rach.'

That's something I really like about Dad. Once you've got him to listen he always takes your ideas seriously. He never makes fun of them—however crazy they sound.

'*Theoretically*, it's possible,' he says. 'But it's a big leap to make, a very big leap. I haven't even proved that skyberries can affect rabbits yet. But people . . . '

I can tell he's giving it some thought though. Then suddenly, his eyes dart away over the dunes. He's spotted another rabbit.

Oh no. I've just thought of something myself.

Oh no, oh no, oh no.

'Try to ignore it, Rach,' I whisper, inside my head.

But it's no good. I've gone and thought of it now. And it annihilates my idea about the islanders being compass brains. Kills it stone dead.

'I've just thought of something, Dad.'

My voice sounds really squashed and miserable. But I can't help it. I loved that idea. It made me feel clever, like I knew some answers for a change. 'You know Mistress Lodesman?'

He shakes his head. 'I don't *know* her. I've *heard* about her. Was she the teacher here before your mum?'

'That's right. She lives on Wreckers' Point and she's got blue hair and she's got her great-great-grandad Asa Lodesman's uniform hanging on her wall because she thinks he was a great pilot and it wasn't his fault that the *Mary Ellen* got wrecked and all those people got drowned. And she's the Go-Between and the skyberry wine maker.'

Dad looks really baffled. 'You've lost me there, Rach.' He's sliding his computer out of his pocket.

'Well, never mind that last bit. But, anyway, the point is—she never touches skyberries. Alban told me. She doesn't like them. But she can home. I saw her once walking in the estuary in the thick fog. And she didn't drown or get lost. She knew exactly which direction to go in. So if she never eats skyberries she shouldn't be a compass head, should she? But she *is*. I saw her homing. So that proves my idea's crap, doesn't it?'

A minute ago I was dead sure I was right. But I'm all confused again now.

It's as if Pilot Island is going, 'Ha, ha, ha! Nice try! But you mainlanders can't find out our secrets *that* easily.'

Dad nods slowly. He doesn't want to trash my idea completely. He's got this big respect for ideas. He just says, 'The place to start is with these rabbits. Proving a direct link between their behaviour and skyberries. That's what we have to concentrate on. If I can prove that . . . '

He picks up some bright blue bunny poo and crumbles it between his fingers and sniffs it.

'Bye, Dad.'

I start walking away. But I turn round to take one last look.

The rabbits are coming out of their holes. Creeping up to him now that I've gone. They're not scared at all. They're so close he could touch them. They're sitting in rows, like an audience, while he types into his computer. And they're all facing due north.

'Bye, Dad.'

But he doesn't hear me.

I forgot about the fog. On the way round to Wreckers' Point it comes rolling sneakily out of the dunes. At first I don't even notice because I'm thinking.

Not about the secrets of Pilot Island because that gives me brain-ache.

Not about Alban because that makes me sad. I might as well admit it—there's no future in me and Alban is there? When I'm at school on the mainland and he's stuck on Pilot Island and he can't ever leave because it makes him so sick? We might as well be on different planets. I can't even phone him for a chat.

'Forget about him, Rach!' says a stern voice inside my head. 'Think about something cheery!'

So I start thinking about electricity. Our electricity comes on today. Not long now—that's what the men said who are fixing up our wind turbine. One of them said to me, 'Just a few more hours and you'll be listening to your CDs.'

Now, that's *really* cheery. I can listen to my CDs, fix myself some Micro Chips, watch my telly programmes, and dry my hair with my hairdrier. All at the same time if I feel like it. Things'll be *normal* again. Well, as normal as they ever get on Pilot Island.

I'm at the burnt-out house where the last warden lived before I notice the fog. But by then it's creeping up all around me. And it's far too late to escape.

10

Lost in the fog. It's my worst nightmare. All the times I've dreamed about this, I can't believe that I've let it happen again for real. But here I am with my shadow and the sun hot on my back. Shut in by white mist that moves and twists all around me.

Straightaway my sense of direction goes. The only real thing is the shells crunching like cornflakes under my feet. You can't trust anything else. Your eyes are no good because the fog plays tricks on them. You think you see a rock then it just dissolves. Your ears are no good because sounds get all confused. You think something's really close and it's miles away, on the mainland.

I just panic. My heart's going *boom, boom, boom* and I'm breathing faster and faster and whirling about this way, that way. But everywhere I turn there's thick white cloud as if I'm lost in the sky.

The last warden, the engineer, Asa Lodesman—it's like their ghosts are in the fog with me. As if, when they drowned, they became part of the fog that's going to drown me now.

'Help! Help!'

I'm shouting even though I know it's hopeless. Who's going to hear me? I'm on the wrong side of the island. The islanders and their fishing boats and the oyster beds are round the other side. No one but Mistress Lodesman lives on Wreckers' Point.

But I still go on shouting.

Something's tugging my feet. Horror flashes right

through me—like an electric shock. I daren't look down. I've got to.

The mud has sucked in my shoes and the sea is licking my ankles. It's got me. Pilot Island has got me. I knew it would, in the end.

This time my voice is a scream of despair. It doesn't even sound human.

'Help meeee!'

Slurp, slurp, the mud makes gurgling sounds when I pull one shoe out. But as soon as I put it down it's swallowed again. Cold waves are creeping up to my knees.

'Help me. I'm drowning!'

Slap, slap, slap. What's that? My ears are playing tricks.

Slap, slap, slap. No they're not. I can feel hope fizzing inside me like lemonade. Because I know that sound. The sound of leather sandals on wet sand.

'Rachel?'

'I'm over here!'

Didn't think I'd ever be glad to see that stern face and that blue waterfall hair. Mistress Lodesman comes marching out of the fog like she's taking a morning walk. I can feel my face sliding into a big sloppy grin. I'm all right now. She can home. There's nothing to be scared of now.

Her hair is more like a waterfall than ever. It's sparkling with water drops from the fog.

'Get me out of here please, Mistress Lodesman.'

She wades towards me, gives me a long, hard look. But I don't care because I'm safe now she's here.

I can hear the sea rumbling somewhere very close. It sounds like a great big engine. But even that doesn't worry me. I'm with someone who can home. We'll just go strolling out of the fog and end up right outside her cottage at Wreckers' Point.

But she doesn't move. Even though we're both standing knee-deep in the sea and there's no sun any more, not even a yellow blur, and I'm starting to shiver with the dampness and cold.

'Which way is it?' I beg her, grabbing hold of her arm.

'Shhhh!'

She shakes me off. She's holding her face up into the fog.

'What are you *doing*!'

'I'm trying to feel a breeze on my cheek—to guide us towards the island. I'm listening for island sounds. They will guide us there too.'

But there's only a tiny breeze. And the rest of the world could be dead. Because there's no sound coming through the fog. Except for the growling of the sea.

'Shhhh!' she says when I open my mouth to speak. 'We must look for other signs.'

But I won't shush. A thought has just hit me. It's hit me so hard that I'm gasping, like someone's punched me in the stomach.

'Other signs?' I can hardly get the words out. 'What do you need signs for? You can home. You *can* home, can't you?'

She doesn't answer, like she's admitting the terrible truth.

I push my face close to hers and yell at her.

'I can't believe this! You *can't* home, can you? Go on! Why don't you *say* it!'

'No,' she says, after a long, long pause, 'I can't home. I've never had that gift.'

Great. I'm stuck out here with the only islander who can't home. That's really great. I thought I would go hysterical. But I don't. It's like I've got no energy left to panic. Like I've just given up. I can't fight Pilot Island any more.

Still, I can't stay here. I unplug my feet from the mud, one *glug*, two *glugs*, and start dragging my way through the water. Mistress Lodesman follows me.

'No,' she says. 'Not this way, Rachel. You're walking out into the estuary.'

'How do *you* know?'

I spit out the question as if I hate her. But I don't really care about the answer. My legs feel heavy. I just want to lie down somewhere and rest.

'Look at the way the water's flowing, Rachel. Use your eyes. You're walking out to sea.'

'I don't care.'

'Turn your face round,' she orders me. Who does she think she is, giving me orders?

'Rachel, listen to me! Turn your face round. Sniff the air.'

Sniff the air? She's crazy. She must be crazy. So I just carry on staggering round in circles.

I'm cold. My knees start folding up. I'm sinking into the waves. I just want to go to sleep.

'Rachel! Stand to attention! Do it immediately!'

There's something about that teacher-voice that wakes my brain up. I stand up straight like a naughty school-kid. I even sniff the air like she told me to.

'What do you smell, Rachel?'

'Coconut. It's coconut!'

The gorse flowers on Pilot Island smell like coconut. It's wafting out from the dunes. We're not as lost as I thought.

Somewhere inside me there's hope again. I can feel it, light as a bubble. Mistress Lodesman takes my arm and we slosh out of the sea.

We're on slippery mud, then sliding on seaweedy rocks. The fog is thick as ever. It makes your eyes ache trying to see through it.

'I still can't see which way to go!'

But Mistress Lodesman stays icy calm. She crouches down and pulls some seaweed off a rock and shows me it.

'This red seaweed dies,' she says, 'if it dries out too much.'

I can feel myself getting frantic again.

What's wrong with her? She's *definitely* crazy. Telling me about seaweed when the tide's sneaking in all around us. When all the channels are racing with foamy water. Maybe we're already cut off. Maybe—

'That means,' says Mistress Lodesman in her firm clear voice, 'that this mud where we are standing now will be covered soon by the tide. We must move away from here, move towards dry land. So look for brown seaweed.'

The fog still blinds us. So we keep together, taking tiny steps and searching the sand around our feet.

'There's some brown.'

'Excellent,' says Mistress Lodesman like I've come top of the class. 'This seaweed can stay out of the water longer. So it grows further up the shore. We're going in the right direction. We're going towards dry land.'

'Look for chanelled wrack now,' says Mistress Lodesman.

'What's that?' I'm taking notice now. Because, even though she can't home, she seems to know the way.

'It's another kind of seaweed. It looks like long brown twisted ribbons. It only needs to be sprayed with water so it can grow high up on the beach. When we find the chanelled wrack we're almost home.'

So we follow the seaweed to safety. We move slowly through the fog from sea to mud to sand and all the time Mistress Lodesman is listening and sniffing, looking out for signs.

'I can smell the wild roses in the dunes,' she says. 'The wind is stronger. Shhhh, listen, Rachel. You can hear the wind chimes outside my front door.'

I stop trudging along and listen. I listen so hard that my ears hurt.

'I can hear them too!' It's just a far-away tinkling, somewhere in the fog. But I can hear them.

Suddenly, my feet splash into water.

'Mistress Lodesman, there's a channel here. We're going the wrong way. We're walking back out to sea!'

'No, no, Rachel. Taste the water.'

'Taste it?'

I scoop some into my hand, screwing up my face because I know it will be salty.

But when I sip it it's not salty at all. It's *fresh* water.

'And use your eyes,' says Mistress Lodesman. 'Look, this is the last seaweed. The last seaweed we need to look for.'

She pulls some green stuff out of the water. 'It's called sea lettuce. But it grows in fresh water streams that run down to the sea. Like the streams that flow through our dunes.'

It takes a second for this to sink in.

Then I start yelling my head off. 'We're safe! We're back in the dunes!'

'We're safe,' she says in a voice calm as custard. 'And if I've read the signs correctly we should be very near to Wreckers' Point. Sit down, Rachel. We're not in any danger now. Sit down and wait for the fog to clear.'

I sit down, *plonk*, in the sand. I didn't know I could feel so wrecked and weary. For a long time I can't think about anything—it's like my mind's shut down. I just stare at my feet. I can't seem to feel anything either.

But then I notice a warm, soft breeze on my skin and I lift up my head.

The fog's getting wispy. Then the wisps twirl away and there's clear blue sky behind them. I'm not at all surprised where we've ended up. Asa Lodesman's black pilot boat, the *Dove*, is just along the beach. And on the other side is Wreckers' Point, grey and rocky with the stump of the lighthouse on the end of it. Now all we have to do is climb and we're at the door of Mistress Lodesman's house.

Ting, ting, ting, ting.

That's the sound of her wind chimes, up above our heads. It's just some old glass pebbles clinking together. But, to me, it sounds like lovely music.

Mistress Lodesman looks into my face. 'Are you recovered, Rachel?'

'I'm all right.'

I can't forget how she was, out in the fog. How she didn't panic. How she stayed cool and looked for signs and how she probably saved my life.

She doesn't look stern any more, just worn out. Her face looks grey and old. And it hits me, for the first time, that she took a big risk, coming to get me. She can't home. She was in danger out there, just the same as me.

'Thanks,' I say to her awkwardly, 'for coming out to get me.'

And, suddenly, I don't feel scared, after what we've been through, about asking her something personal.

'Mistress Lodesman, can I ask you something? Do the other islanders know that you can't home?'

Her seawater green eyes stare into mine. There's a long wait, as if she's deciding whether to speak. Then she says, 'Perhaps some know. Perhaps some have guessed. I have never been the same as the other islanders. I have never been able to home—I don't know why. But when I was a child I learned to disguise it. I learned to use my other five senses—to watch the movement of the water, to feel the wind, to listen for sounds. And that was usually good enough. Except for today. I thought we might have been lost out there today.'

And she stares out over the estuary. It's sparkling now with frilly waves. But the places where we walked are under deep water.

I don't need to ask her why she faked being able to home. I already know. I know what it's like being different on Pilot Island, not being able to join in with the other kids.

But she says, as if she's reading my mind, 'Once I'd started pretending, I couldn't stop. I come from a proud family—all of the Lodesmans, like my great-great-grandfather, were famous navigators. To have a daughter who couldn't home . . . ' Mistress Lodesman shrugs and sighs. 'It would not matter now who knew it. But I keep up the pretence. Perhaps you might think I am a stupid, proud old woman.'

'No, never,' I tell her. And I'm not lying or trying to grease round her or anything. 'I'd never think that.'

We climb up through the yellow gorse. I think I'll always remember that sweet coconut smell.

Then we're in the cool blue glow of Mistress Lodesman's cottage.

'Would you like some skyberry juice?' She takes down a bottle from a shelf.

'No thanks,' I shake my head. 'I don't like skyberries. Stevie's mad keen on them. But I don't like them.'

My legs are shaking. That's crazy, isn't it? I go through all that danger. And they decide to shake now that I'm safe. If I press my knees together maybe I can stop them.

And something's itching in my head. It's bothering me. It's something to do with homing and rabbits and skyberries and Mistress Lodesman. To do with what Dad was saying this morning in the dunes. That was only an hour ago but it seems like days. My brain's not working properly yet. It doesn't want to remember. It's having a rest from thinking.

Then something Mistress Lodesman says gets it thinking again. Not about rabbits—about something completely different.

I must have been staring at Asa Lodesman's uniform on the wall. I didn't mean to—I wasn't even seeing it.

But Mistress Lodesman says, 'I see you are looking at the uniform, Rachel. Alban told me you had read something. You had read that he was a villain and got drunk and piloted the pleasure boat on to the rocks. And because of his disgrace the whole island suffered.'

'Errr, well, yes. Mum got this old book, from a second-hand shop . . . '

I feel really awkward. I don't know what to say. Before she saved me it would have given me a buzz to embarrass her about her grandad. I thought she was a snotty old woman then. But not now. 'It didn't actually *say* he was a villain or anything . . . ' I tell her.

'Ah, but that's what people thought, you see. He was branded a criminal, a murderer. They wanted to put him in chains! Undeserved,' she says, her eyes shining like jewels. 'Undeserved, Rachel! And one day I shall prove how unjustly Asa Lodesman was treated. He was not responsible for the deaths of those poor people. It casts a shadow on the whole island, not only on our family. It was a terrible injustice. It's my duty to right it. And if I cannot right it, one day, perhaps after I am dead, someone will right it for me.'

You know what I'm thinking to myself? I'm thinking: She sounds a little bit crazy, talking like this.

But, big surprise, it doesn't worry me. If she wants to get fired up about her great-great-grandad's reputation, then so what? She's allowed.

Because I've decided I like her. And once I like someone I don't let anyone disrespect them. Look what she did. She can't home but she came into the fog to save me. She risked her life for me, a mainlander. Far as I'm concerned she can go on about Asa Lodesman as much as she likes.

And I think she *would* have gone on and on talking about injustices and undeserved and stuff like that. Only, just as she's starting up again, Alban comes into the cottage.

'Mistress Lodesman, are you at home? I've got some skyberries for you.'

11

I haven't seen Alban since we went to the mainland
together. Oh yes, I have. I forgot—I saw him running
around last night in the storm. His eyes aren't wild like
they were then. They're calm seawater green. Except he
looks a bit embarrassed at seeing me.

He's stopped wearing his mainland clothes. He's got
his island clothes on again—that saggy orange jumper
and baggy corduroy trousers.

He mumbles 'Hello' at me as if he's shy.

I'm not shy. I've never been shy in my life. So I say,
straight out, 'Saw you last night, outside our house on the
beach.'

I feel quite chatty now I've got over being lost in the
fog. In fact I want to talk. I've hardly talked to anyone
since we moved to Pilot Island. I'm friends with them
now. Mum would be proud of me. Mistress Lodesman has
been telling me all sorts of private stuff. She told me she
can't home, didn't she? And even the other islanders don't
know that. But she told *me*.

So it's OK to ask them anything I like.

'What was going on last night, out in the storm? Were
you there, Mistress Lodesman? I saw Alban and Stevie but
I didn't see you. What were you all doing on the beach?
I thought at first you were collecting sea coal but then it
looked like you were all going crazy to me, running
around in circles, getting soaked to the skin.'

I'm talking too much. I think I've said something wrong
because when I stop to take a breath they're not looking
at me. They're looking at each other behind my back with

quick sideways glances. I know what that means. Secrets again. Something only the islanders know. Something we've got to keep from the mainlander, from the stranger. And I really thought I wasn't a stranger any more.

Stupid, stupid, stupid.

It makes me so confused and angry being shut out again that I can't bear to stay there a minute longer. So I just blurt out some excuse: 'Got to go. Got to listen to my CDs.'

And I rush out the door without even seeing the expression on their faces.

Someone's shouting, 'Rachel, wait!' behind me.

It sounds like Alban. But that just makes me run even faster through the dunes. Smashing down the skyberry bushes, splashing through the lettuce seaweed in a freshwater stream.

There's that coconut smell in my nose—I hate it now. Thorny branches are ripping my clothes but I don't care. I just run and run until there are red stars exploding in my head and my lungs are on fire and I can't . . . run . . . any more.

And all the time I'm panting, 'To hell with them to hell with them to hell with them,' until I collapse half-way up a sand dune.

There's something prickling in my eyes. It must be sand, it can't be tears. I never cry.

'TO HELL WITH THEM!' I roar out one last time. And that makes me feel a lot better.

I even feel hungry. I haven't had any lunch yet. And it's already nearly tea time.

'Who was that shouting just then?' says a voice. 'Was that you, Rach?'

It's Stevie, tramping through the sand dunes chewing skyberries like he's chewing gum.

For once he's without Red Fish and his other little pals. But he's probably on his way to meet them. Usually, I've got loads of patience with Stevie. But today the sight of him with his blue skyberry lips and skyberry friendship bands really gets on my nerves. I don't care if I upset him.

I even *want* to upset him.

'Think you're great now, don't you?'

'What?' He stops chewing and looks surprised.

'Think you're better than the rest of us now you're an islander, don't you?'

'You mad with me or something, Rach?' he says. He rips off a blade of grass and blows on it so it makes a screechy sound.

'Stop doing that!'

'Sounds like an owl, doesn't it? Alban showed me.'

'Well, it gets on my nerves!'

He shrugs. 'OK,' and lets the grass drop onto the sand.

The calmer he is, the madder I get. On the mainland it used to be the other way round.

I can feel myself losing control but today I don't care. All the hard, spiky feelings shut up deep inside me come bursting out into the light. *Pow, pow, pow,* I throw them at Stevie like I'm throwing death stars.

'Suppose you think you're great now, swaggering round like you're Mr Important? Like you're Lord of Pilot Island? Even Mistress Lodesman knows who you are! And stop looking at me like you're sorry for me. How dare you look at me like that? Who do you think you are? It was different on the mainland, wasn't it? Oh yeah. You needed me to tie your shoe-laces, protect you from the bad boys. Well, guess what? I got sick of it. Yes I did! Sick of you getting all the attention: "Oh, we mustn't upset Stevie." Sick of you being such a drag. So what do you think about that, eh?'

The words come spitting out of my mouth like poison. I'm really shocked, I shouldn't talk to Stevie like that. I should hate myself. But I don't. I'm even *glad* I said it. If Stevie had stayed cool as a cucumber, I'd probably have given him a good slap as well. That's something else I should *never* do. Because Stevie is too clumsy to defend himself. He doesn't stand a chance in fights. But I might have hit him anyway.

Only Stevie doesn't stay cool. The old mainland Stevie comes flashing back into his eyes. He scowls. His face goes red and ugly and he starts yelling:

'You hate it don't you, Rach, because I've got my own friends? You can't stand it 'cos you can't interfere. Well, I got sick of you interfering, sick of you treating me like a retard. Sick of you always being around tying my shoe-laces. So there! Yah!' And he sticks out his tongue at me. His tongue is bright blue.

'Retard, my bottom! I never treated you like a retard.'

'Yes you did, yes you did, yes you did!'

So we're standing there, making evil eyes at each other and panting like we've been in a real fight. And I can see from his face that he's as shocked and thrilled at the words coming out of his mouth as I was.

Then, suddenly, I don't want to yell any more. I just feel so weary and my arms and legs feel floppy and I want to lie down and rest. So I do. I go *plonk* into the middle of some skyberry bushes. The blue berries come pitter-pattering down all around me. I close my eyes.

Stevie says, 'You all right, Rach? Look, I'm sorry I said them things about you. I never meant them, honest.'

'Yes you did,' I tell him with my eyes still closed. My voice isn't angry. It's just sad.

Suppose I should feel angry. Especially when he said that I treated him like a retard. Other people did that. Not me. But I don't feel angry. I haven't got the energy. I just feel tired and empty inside like all my anger has washed away.

I open my eyes again. The sky over my head is very blue, full of fat, fluffy clouds.

'Let's not fight, Stevie. I shouldn't have said what I did, either. I don't know what's the matter with me.'

Suddenly Stevie looks sly and says something I'm not expecting. 'That Alban fancies you,' he says, grinning.

'What?'

'He really likes you. He told me. He's always asking me things about you. Soppy things, like what's your favourite colour and stuff.'

'Did he tell you he liked me. Honest?' I'm really surprised and curious. 'What else did he say?'

Stevie shrugs. 'He said, "I like your sister." '

'Is that all? What did he ask you about me? What did you say my favourite colour was?'

'I said pink.'

'I hate pink—it's yukky. You know I do! What did you tell him that for? I like white, or blue.'

'He said lots of other stuff. But I can't remember, it was too soppy.'

'Stevie, I could strangle you.'

But he knows I don't mean it. There's a smile trapped inside me. And any second it's going to break out all over my face.

Stevie makes big smacking noises with his lips. *'Mwaa! Mwaa!* That's you and Alban kissing. *Tee, hee, hee!'* he says, giggling, with his hand stuffed over his mouth.

'Clear off, you menace!' I yell at him. But I'm only joking.

He sticks out his blue tongue at me so I pelt him with

skyberries. He skips about trying to dodge them but of course they hit him every time. 'Go on, clear off!'

He shuffles off, laughing like mad. I'm laughing too.

But at the back of my mind there's a shadow. It won't go away—those words we shouted at each other. It's made a difference. Things have changed somehow. But I don't want to think about it now. I'll think about it later.

I can't think about it now anyway. Because there's Dad, crawling round a sand dune.

'Hi, Dad!'

I'm pleased to see him. It's been a really rough day so far. If I'd known I would have stayed in bed, just taking it easy, until the electricity came. But Dad will take my mind off it. He'll talk about rabbits and skyberries and things that only matter to wildlife wardens. Things a kid doesn't have to worry about.

'What are you doing, Dad?'

'Shhh, Rach, don't make a noise. You'll frighten the rabbits.'

He stretches out on his stomach among the skyberry bushes. So I lie down beside him and whisper into his ear. 'What you doing, Dad? What's that you've got?'

He's got some kind of gadget on the sand beside him. It's just a flat piece of wood with a coil of orange wire on top of it. And the ends of the wire are connected up to a battery.

Dad whispers back at me. 'It's an electro-magnet, Rach. Home-made. Copper wire wound round an iron nail. So when I switch it on, there's an electric current flowing through the wire. It's a bit crude. But it should do the job.'

'What job? What you talking about?'

'Shhh. Stay still.'

There's a rabbit creeping out of its burrow. It's nibbling the grass, its nose twitching.

Dad waits. He puts a warning hand on my arm so I don't move. I'm getting cramp in my legs, I don't like waiting. But we have to wait some more.

The rabbit hops towards our hiding place. We could almost touch it. It stretches out on the warm sand, closing its eyes. It's sunbathing. It's so peaceful.

'See, Rach, see how it's lying. North to south,' murmurs Dad out of the corner of his mouth.

Then very, very sneakily, he slides the electro-magnet thing along the sand until it's close to the rabbit's head and his finger presses down some kind of lever.

The rabbit's eyes shoot open. It shakes its head about.

Dad's fingers tap up and down on the lever.

The rabbit goes berserk. It bucks up and down like a little pony. Its eyes are wild and terrified. It's staggering round in crazy circles. Dad's not even bothering to hide himself now. He's crouching next to the rabbit, working the electro-magnet, switching the current on and off. But the rabbit doesn't seem to know that he's there. It's twitching like it's in a fit, dragging itself round in the grass.

I can't bear to see it suffering like that. Its eyes are rolling. It's really sick. And suddenly, in a flash of awful memory, I think of Alban and Stevie on the mainland.

'Turn it off, Dad!'

Dad lifts his finger off the lever. 'It worked, Rach. My experiment worked. Look, it's OK. The rabbit's not hurt.'

I can't believe my eyes. The rabbit just shakes its head, once, twice. Then it hops away and starts nibbling the grass. As if nothing had happened.

Dad's really excited. 'Rach, you know I said about these rabbits having magnetic particles in their brains? And how I didn't have the right equipment to prove it?'

I nod but don't say anything. I'm not thinking about rabbits—I'm thinking about people. Inside my head these dreadful thoughts are hatching out like monsters. I want to stop them but I can't.

But all Dad can think about is his rabbit experiment. 'See, this is what was happening, Rach.'

He feels about in the pocket of his camouflage jacket and pulls out a little compass. He steadies it on his palm until the needle settles north to south.

'Now watch this—when I put an electric current near it.'

He gives the compass a quick burst of electricity from the electro-magnet and *whizz*, the needle swings around. He switches off the electricity and the needle goes back, wobbles a bit, then settles north/south like it was before.

'Magnetic fields, see, Rachel. Didn't you do this at school? Didn't you learn how any wire that carries an electric current has a magnetic field around it?'

'Er, yeah, we might have.'

'Well, the rabbits eat skyberries, right? So they've got magnetic particles in their brain that act like little compasses?'

'Right.'

'So the little compasses in their brains have got their own magnetic field. But I can make a *stronger* magnetic field than theirs by using electricity. With my electro-magnet.'

He waves the electro-magnet at me just to make quite sure I understand.

'So I come along with my electro-magnet and turn it on and *pow!* my stronger magnetic field scrambles up the magnetic field in their brain. Just like you saw it scrambling that compass needle just now. And they get disorientated and run around in circles and get dizzy and fall over. And when I turn it off, hey presto, their brains go back to normal and they're OK.'

Those monsters are growing fast.

'So I was right all along,' says Dad grinning at how clever he's been. 'They *have* got a sixth sense. They *have* got compasses in their heads. Because if they didn't this gadget wouldn't affect them one bit.'

'Dad,' I interrupt him, pulling at his sleeve. 'Dad.'

'You know where I got this idea from, Rach? To do the experiment with electricity? It was from my computer. I left it switched on, in the grass, and I noticed the rabbits didn't like it. They got agitated near it. And I thought, I bet it's the electricity they don't like. But I needed something more powerful, with a stronger magnetic field, so I made my little electro-magnet. Good, eh? Did you see the way that rabbit's behaviour changed? With just a little *zizz* of electricity? It went crazy!'

Electricity. Suddenly, pieces began falling into place, like someone's doing a jigsaw puzzle inside my head.

Electricity.

'Dad, you've got to listen to me, Dad.'

'What, Rachel. What?'

He looks into my face for the first time.

'I think the Pilot Islanders go mad with electricity too.'

I can't talk fast enough. I'm remembering all sorts of things that didn't make sense then but that make sense now.

'Alban and Stevie don't like my personal stereo, Dad. And there's electricity in that, from the batteries, isn't there? When I put the headphones on their heads they said, "Take it away!" They said it hurt their heads.'

Dad says, without thinking, 'There are tiny electro-magnets inside stereo headphones.'

'Well, no *wonder* it hurt them, then. And don't you see,

Dad, the electricity hurt them because they eat skyberries and they're compass-heads. Just like the rabbits.'

There are other things too, other things about electricity, fizzing around in my brain but I haven't got time to connect them up because Dad says, 'Whoa there, Rach. Whoa!! All this stuff about the islanders having compasses in their heads. I thought we'd decided that was going too far. What about that woman? What was her name— Mistress Lodesman? The one who didn't eat skyberries and could still home . . . ?'

'Mistress Lodesman can't home, Dad. I know that for sure. I got lost in the fog and she couldn't home. She found her way by the seaweed.'

For a split second I wonder if it's OK to tell about Mistress Lodesman not being able to home. But she didn't say it was a secret or anything, did she? And I'm only telling my dad, not any of the islanders.

Dad scrunches up his face. 'Are you certain about this?'

'She told me herself. Actually, at first she didn't tell me. I guessed. But then she told me I'd guessed right.'

'That makes things a lot more complicated,' is all Dad says. 'A lot more complicated.' He sounds really doubtful, like he's not convinced. But his eyes are far-away. He's thinking hard.

I'm thinking too. I've just thought of something else. 'Lightning is electricity, isn't it?'

Dad nods.

'I saw them in the storm. The island people. When the lightning came and it was going *flash, flash* every minute, they all came pouring out from behind the high walls. They were sort of wild, running about like headless chickens. Stevie was with them. Stevie's a compass-head too, you know.'

Dad looks serious now. He looks deadly serious. He stays quiet for a long time, staring into the distance. Then he says, 'Stevie can't go to the mainland, Rach. Remember what happened, when we tried to go there?'

'Yes, but I don't understand about that. Alban was like that. I told you in the jeep but you weren't listening. I tried to take Alban to the mainland and we got to the exact same spot and he got really sick, he had a sort of fit and Mistress Lodesman rescued him. I don't understand why he did that.'

'I do,' says Dad. 'It was the pylons. Didn't you see them, Rach? There are massive pylons in the fields on either side and where Stevie got sick, you have to go under the cables. The magnetic field from pylons is really powerful. It would make them really, really ill. It all fits together. And this Mistress Lodesman isn't affected by electricity? She can go to the mainland and not get sick?'

'She's the Go-Between, she goes there all the time. And she's got a computer like yours in her cottage. That doesn't make her sick either. So that's more proof, isn't it?'

Dad shakes his head in amazement. Then he says, 'There needs to be lots more scientific investigation though.'

'Why? It seems simple to me. They're all compass-heads, except for Mistress Lodesman. And electricity scrambles their brains.'

'Yes, that's about it.' But Dad doesn't look pleased that we've worked it all out. He's chewing his lip. He looks really, really worried.

'What are you thinking about now?'

'I'm thinking about the last warden,' says Dad. 'About the night she turned her electricity on for the first time. That was the night her house burnt down. The night she died.'

'Come on, you don't think the islanders had anything to do with that?'

But even when I'm saying it, I'm remembering the engineer and the electric lighthouse. The one that got switched on and burnt down the same night. I wonder if Dad knows about that? It's history and Dad isn't much interested in history. Wildlife is his main thing.

'You don't think they did it, do you, Dad? I mean, they're peaceful and non-violent and stuff. They wouldn't hurt a fly. Everyone knows that.'

'I don't know,' says Dad, chewing his lip a bit more. 'If this is all true, then electricity will disturb the balance of their brains. It'll be like torture to them. They'll do anything to shut it off. They won't be able to help themselves.'

He doesn't need to spell it out. Today is the day *we* get electricity.

And I thought the only thing I'd have to worry about is which CD to play first.

'We'd better go and get Mum,' Dad says, his voice suddenly urgent. 'She's in the schoolhouse.'

'No wait, Dad. When did the men say everything would be set up. You know, for our electricity to come on?'

Dad frowns, looks at his watch. 'It's four o'clock now. They said six o'clock. They have to be gone by then or they won't get back to the mainland. The tide's already coming in. But I don't know, Rach,' says Dad, shaking his head. 'We might be barking up the wrong tree here. We might have got this totally wrong.'

'Then let's go and see Mistress Lodesman. Quick, before six o'clock. She knows all the secrets of Pilot Island. She'll know the truth.'

12

On the way over to Wreckers' Point I decide to warn Dad about Mistress Lodesman. Just in case he gets the wrong idea about her. Just in case he doesn't give her enough respect. That would really show me up.

'She looks a bit weird, Dad, a bit witchy. So don't look surprised or anything.'

Dad just grunts as we go hurrying through the dunes.

'And she wears this old grey dress like a bag-lady. But people respect her. OK? Are you listening, Dad? Look, Dad, there she is.'

Mistress Lodesman is at the end of Wreckers' Point. She's sitting by the electric lighthouse. It's her favourite look-out spot. Asa Lodesman's brass telescope is beside her on the rock. Even from here I can see it flashing gold in the sun.

I thought Alban might still be with her. At least, I hoped he would. But she's alone. I can't see Alban anywhere. He must have gone back home. I can't help it—I know we're on an urgent mission to find out information—but I feel a little twist of sadness in my heart.

Mistress Lodesman picks up the telescope and spies through it at the estuary.

There's patchy fog out there. Like little clouds have fallen out of the sky and are floating on the water. The tide is coming in fast. There's still dry land by the poles—a strip of mud maybe half a mile wide. That'll be the last thing to go under. But when it does the only way to get to the mainland will be by boat.

Dad and me are rushing past the *Dove*. He hardly looks at her. But I do. I crane my neck to look up her high black sides until I can see the deck.

'Alban?' I thought he might be aboard her, with a tin of black paint or something. But no one comes to the side of the *Dove* and looks down. And then I feel like a fool for shouting out his name.

'Have you been round here before?' I ask my dad after I've panted to catch up with him. 'Have you seen Mistress Lodesman's cottage and the lighthouse and the *Dove*?'

Dad gives a quick, impatient nod which I guess means, yes he has. Then he says, 'The more I think about all this the scarier it gets. I really hope we're wrong about the islanders, Rach. I really hope that skyberries only affect birds and rabbits.'

The rock is seaweedy and slippery. Dad and me scramble up it until we're on top of Wreckers' Point.

Mistress Lodesman doesn't turn round. But I know she knows we're here. She probably saw us coming from a long way off. And if she didn't, she heard us. The first tinkling pebble that slipped down when we were climbing—I bet she heard it. With her extra-sharp five senses she probably smelt my 'Blossom' body spray. It smells lovely, like a bunch of flowers.

When we're very close to her she puts the telescope down and stands up to meet us.

I needn't have warned Dad about her looking witchy. Because she doesn't actually. Her blue waterfall hair is tidied back into a long plait.

'Mistress Lodesman, this is my dad.' I point Dad out to her, as if there were crowds of people on the rock to choose from, not just him.

Mistress Lodesman's face is calm but a little bit curious. 'I've seen your father often,' she says, 'out on the dunes.'

Dad nods at her, 'Mistress Lodesman.' He sounds very polite, very respectful. Good.

My dad's a wow with rabbits but he's shy with people. I can see he's shy of Mistress Lodesman. Well, anybody would be—with her blue hair and sea-green eyes that seem to look right through you.

But I'm not shy of her, not since we found our way out of the fog together. Not since I found out that she can't home either.

Only problem is, I don't know where to start asking questions. So I just blurt out the first thing that comes into my head.

'Mistress Lodesman, I was looking out the window last night. It was really late. And there was this storm. Look.' I point down to the beach to show her the stuff the storm washed up—nets and broken fishing boxes and all sorts of rubbish. 'It was really bad. Did you hear it?'

She doesn't nod or say anything. She just watches me with those X-ray eyes. But I manage to carry on.

'Anyhow . . . anyhow, when I looked out the window I saw the island people. Alban was with them. Even Stevie my brother was. The thing is, they were wandering round like they were crazy or something—or sick or something.'

I stop—then realize I haven't asked her a question yet. But it's OK because Dad takes over. He's forgotten about being shy. 'Mistress Lodesman,' he says in a grim voice. 'Do the islanders often have episodes like that? Where their behaviour changes? Where they become really agitated and disorientated?'

Mistress Lodesman still doesn't say anything. But then Dad really surprises me by asking straight out, not shy at all. 'Did it happen on the night the last warden died? Did they burn down her house? Did they chase her into the estuary where she drowned? Did they even kill her?'

There's a long, long silence while we all look at each other. Maybe it's only me who feels icy-cold even though the sun is blazing down on us.

'Please tell us,' Dad says to Mistress Lodesman. 'It's very important for us to know what we're dealing with.'

'And if it's a secret we'll keep it a secret,' I tell her because I know more about Pilot Island than Dad does. I know it doesn't like mainlanders knowing its secrets.

Mistress Lodesman frowns. Then she sighs. 'I suppose it had to be told sometime,' she says. 'Even though it's a shameful thing.'

She plonks herself down on a rock again as if she's suddenly very tired. I almost ask if she's OK because I've just remembered after she saved Alban when she put a hand to her chest as if her heart hurt her. But it's too late. She's already started to speak.

'The islanders would not deliberately harm anyone. But when the sickness comes, they are not in their right minds. They started to burn her house. They didn't harm her but the poor young woman was frightened. She ran out into the estuary. It was a terrible thing, a shameful thing. I tried to stop them but that night they were very sick.'

'Like they were in the storm?' I ask her. When I say it I can see them in my mind. How they were in the storm with their crazy, frightened eyes.

'Much worse than that,' says Mistress Lodesman, closing her eyes as if she can't bear to remember. 'Sometimes if the sickness comes slowly they bar the gates. They shut themselves in so they cannot roam outside the walls. But that night it came very swiftly. I tried to stop them, to bar the gates. But I didn't have the strength.'

There's something I need to know about the night the last warden died. It's been troubling me for a long time.

'Why didn't the islanders save her? If they didn't want to hurt her, why didn't they just go out into the fog and bring her back?'

'You don't understand,' says Mistress Lodesman, shaking her head sadly. 'When the sickness happens they cannot home. They become wild, unpredictable. Like different people.'

'How often does this sickness happen?' Dad wants to know. 'And why does it happen? Have you any ideas about that?'

'I read a book,' I chip in, 'about the electric lighthouse.' I kick out at a granite block so she knows which lighthouse I'm talking about. 'This got burnt down as well, didn't it? Did the islanders do that?'

Mistress Lodesman just looks upset like we're crowding her with too many questions. 'Wait,' she says in a tired voice. 'These are very grave matters. Difficult to speak of. You must give me time.'

'Sorry, Mistress Lodesman,' says Dad, checking his watch. 'But there may not be much time.'

Mistress Lodesman takes a deep breath, like she's made a decision.

'It happens very rarely,' she says. 'And as to why it happens . . . storms affect them. But on the night the last warden died there was no storm at all. Yet that night the sickness drove them almost mad. So I have no ideas. There seems to be no link . . . '

I open my mouth to say, 'Electricity,' but Dad waves me to be quiet. He wants to hear her out.

'And about the lighthouse, Rachel, I cannot say. It happened too long ago. There was a story on the mainland that the islanders burnt it down and drowned the keeper out of malice. But that is not true. We have no malice towards mainlanders. We must keep ourselves separate, that's all. And now you know why. Those high walls are not to keep the mainlanders out. They are to keep us in.'

There's something else I've got to ask. Even though I might not want to hear the answer. 'When they burnt down the warden's house, was Alban there. Was he?'

Mistress Lodesman looks sad and sorry. 'He was. But remember, Rachel, when the sickness comes, they cannot help what they do. Afterwards some don't remember. Some half-remember and it makes them very wretched.'

Dad's looking more and more grim-faced. 'But you never get this sickness?' he asks Mistress Lodesman. 'Not in a storm? Not at any time?'

'No,' says Mistress Lodesman. 'My head stays clear. And again, I cannot see why I should be different.'

'I think we know,' says Dad.

And finally he tells her—about the others being compass-heads. And then he tells her about the electricity. And how it drives compass people crazy.

And then the last thing he says is, 'So we've come to ask you. Are we wrong here? Do you have any other explanation that proves we're wrong?'

You can tell by his voice—he wants her to say, 'You're a zillion miles from the truth, pal!' But she doesn't. Instead she says, as if we've given her some really great news, 'Electricity! I didn't think of that.'

But she's thinking fast now.

And after a while she says, in an excited voice, 'But I believe that you are right. Electricity is the link. Electricity is what brings on the sickness. And that is what happened aboard the *Mary Ellen* the day of the tragedy. I *knew* my great-great-grandfather was not guilty. And they wanted to take him away in chains! Rachel, the *Mary Ellen* had an *electric* motor! So my grandfather could not navigate. He was not a murderer, Rachel. He had the sickness because of the electricity. He was the very first of us to have the sickness!'

Dad's looking totally bewildered. His eyebrows have shot sky-high and he's got an expression on his face that says: 'What's she talking about now!'

But I know. I'm right there with Mistress Lodesman. Asa Lodesman was a compass-head like the rest of them. And he was probably the first compass-head to have his brain messed up with electricity.

'This is a truly wonderful day!' Mistress Lodesman is saying to Dad with her eyes shining. 'Thank you, thank you so much!'

Her face lights up in a brilliant smile and she grabs Dad's hands to thank him. He jumps away—like I said before, he isn't used to people. He hasn't got a clue what's going on. He looks helplessly in my direction so I start to explain: 'Asa Lodesman was Mistress Lodesman's great-great-grandad, and . . . '

I'm just getting into the story when Mistress Lodesman says, 'What is that white van out there, going towards the mainland?'

We all stare out into the estuary. The sun is still shining here. But out there it looks dark—a dirty grey fog is rolling in. You can just see a white van throwing up spray, speeding towards the mainland. Its headlights are two yellow tunnels in the fog.

'My God,' says Dad, 'it's their van. The men who were fixing our wind turbine. They're on their way back home. They must have finished early.'

'Wait,' says Mistress Lodesman. 'I see something else unfamiliar.'

She puts the telescope to her eye. But you don't need a telescope to see it. It's a strange white glow. Like an alien spacecraft has just landed in the dunes.

'It's our house,' whispers Dad. He's got this appalled look on his face. 'The electricity's on already. Every window is lit up. Your mum must be home.'

I feel queasy and I think for one panicky second that I've got the sickness. Then I remember that I don't eat skyberries. So it must be that I'm only scared.

Dad says in an urgent voice, 'Where's Stevie, Rachel? Do you know where he is? Is he at home or with the islanders?'

'I . . . I don't know, Dad. I saw him in the sand dunes not long ago. I think he was going to see his mates.'

'Go after him,' says Dad. 'Bring him home. Before he gets into any trouble.'

He can't take his eyes off our house, all lit up like a Christmas tree.

'What you going to do, Dad?'

'I'm going back to the house, turn off that electricity. The whole house is like a giant magnetic field. God knows what it'll do to their brains. I don't know, maybe they're not sensitive enough to feel it at this distance.'

'I think they are, Dad. Look down there.'

Two island women are walking along the beach. You can see straightaway that they've got the sickness. Or the first stages of it, anyway. They're carrying baskets full of fat purple mussels. They must have picked them off the rocks round Wreckers' Point. But now they've stopped picking mussels. They're stumbling along with a dazed look on their faces. The mussels are spilling out of their baskets but they don't care. They just crunch right over them. They're heading into the dunes, towards the bright white lights of our house.

120

'Why doesn't Mum just turn the electricity off?' I wail at Dad. 'Just turn it off. And the compass-heads won't get sick.'

'But she doesn't know that, does she, Rach?'

Dad's voice sounds snappy and bad-tempered. That's because he's scared, just like I am. 'She doesn't know about the electricity. I didn't know about it myself before today. That's why I've got to get back there and tell her. You find Stevie. Bring him home before he gets himself involved with these compass-heads.'

He must be frantic or he'd never call the islanders compass-heads. That's my name for them.

Anyhow, for a second I stare at him with my mouth open. Has he forgotten? His precious son is a compass-head. And if they're going to burn our house down, like they did the last warden's, he'll probably be right there with them, dancing round the flames.

But Dad's gone before I can say anything. He's not going round by the beach. He's taken the short cut through the dunes. I can see his long, skinny figure crashing through the skyberry bushes. Then he's gone.

Then Mistress Lodesman speaks. I'd almost forgotten she was there. 'Come along, child,' she says in her teacher's voice. 'Come with me. We have work to do. We must try to stop them getting out. We must try to bar the gate.'

13

We're hurrying along by the sea's edge where the sand is firm and it's easier to walk.

Out in the estuary it's getting really dark and gloomy. The fog's still coming in. Not from the dunes but from the open sea. Pilot Island is cut off from the mainland by fog and water. Even the dry land by the poles is under water now. No one from the mainland is coming to help us. No one even knows we're in trouble. We're on our own.

'Mistress Lodesman?'

We haven't spoken to each other since we split up from Dad at Wreckers' Point. But I want Mistress Lodesman to know something. I don't know why it's so urgent to tell her now—when we're racing against time to bar the gates. But it is.

'Mistress Lodesman, I'm really glad to know that your great-great-grandad has got his good name back. I knew all along that he was innocent.'

That's a lie—about knowing he was innocent. I didn't know at all. I didn't much care one way or the other about Asa Lodesman. It's hard to care about some stern old fungus-face who glares at you out of some ancient photo. But I want her to think I cared. So she knows I'm on her side. I've got a lot of time for Mistress Lodesman. Yes, I know I didn't like her at first. In fact, I thought she was a snotty old bag. But I've learned a lot of things about her since then. And I don't even notice her blue hair any more.

Mistress Lodesman just says, 'Thank you, child.'

But she gives me this grateful look, so I know she's got the message.

There's a salty breeze blowing that stings my face. Good weather for windmills. Shit. Why couldn't it have been dead calm?

Bet our wind turbine is whizzing round like a catherine wheel. Bet the generator's pumping out loads of electricity. Bet it's fizzing through cables and wires. You can see our house from here. It's *alive* with electricity. It's like a great big Hallowe'en lantern glowing in the dunes.

Dad should be there soon. Then *click*, he'll kill that electricity stone dead. And the house will go dark. Then the compass-heads will stop getting sick and they'll turn around and go back home and be peaceful fisher-folk again.

We're tramping through the dunes now. It's mega hard work, climbing on sand. I'm panting and hot and sweaty. My hands are covered in bloody scratches where I've pushed my way through the gorse bushes.

'We there yet?'

'At . . . the . . . top . . . of . . . this . . . dune,' gasps Mistress Lodesman.

And there it is, below us—where the islanders live. My stomach's hopping about like a frog—I have to clutch at my middle to make it stop. Because the gates are standing wide open. And there's a gang of islanders already outside the walls.

'We're too late! Look, Mistress Lodesman, they've escaped!'

I search her face for some sign but she just frowns and her lips go tight. 'Not all of them,' she says. 'I see only a few islanders there.'

They're spread out over a wide grassy plain. And they're sick. One of them's doubled over and throwing up. That's just how I feel and I'm not even a compass-head.

Some are stumbling. Some are shaking their heads like they've got wasps in their hair.

The one in the lead isn't stumbling. He's got a blazing torch in his hand. Suddenly he lifts the torch high above his head and I can see who it is. I should have known.

But I can't help whispering his name out loud: 'Alban.'

For a few seconds his face is lit up like a luminous clock—all white and eerie and glowing. It's got blue lips and crazy, staring eyes.

'That's not Alban,' I try to tell myself. 'That freak from a horror film—that's not him.'

But I know it is. 'Rachel, we must hurry,' says Mistress Lodesman, tapping my arm.

'But they'll see us. We have to go past them to bar the gate.'

When they're sick, they're not in their right minds. That's what she said before. I don't want to go past them—I really don't.

'Don't be afraid,' says Mistress Lodesman. 'They are more frightened than we are.'

That's what they say about spiders. I never believed that either.

'And they're in pain,' she says. 'All they want to do is stop the pain. It's the electricity they want to destroy, not us.'

'What if we get in their way?'

But Mistress Lodesman is already on her way down.

It's really weird down there. Weird weather. The sky is packed tight with grey clouds. But behind them the sun is still shining. Because a light, a horrible sickly yellow light, is spilling all over the plain. All over the islanders.

They're collecting together now behind Alban. And they've all turned in the same direction—towards our house. They've located it—the source of the pain.

I go skidding down the dune to catch up with Mistress Lodesman. She's all alone out there—a tiny person, striding across the plain.

But just then Stevie comes out of the open gates. It doesn't look like he's running. He's shuffling along like a boxer with his head down and his elbows stuck out. But I know that he's running at his top speed. He's trying to catch up with Alban and the others.

What Dad told me flashes into my brain: 'Bring Stevie back home. Before he gets into any trouble.'

So I just plant myself in front of him and of course he can't do a body swerve. He just crashes right into me.

He stumbles around a bit, sort of dazed.

Then he says, in a whiny voice, 'Rach, I've got a headache. I need an aspirin.'

He doesn't look too sick yet. He's not howling or dribbling or anything. Not like he was on the mainland when we went under the pylons.

'Stevie, let's go back home. There are aspirins back home. You can have one of those fizzy ones.'

'I've got a fizzy noise in my head.' He slaps his hand against one ear and tilts his head like he's trying to knock the fizziness out the other side.

'It's the skyberries, Stevie. It's the electricity.'

No point in explaining any more. His brain is too scrambled to understand.

'Come on, Stevie.' I grab his arm. 'Dad sent me to fetch you home. You'll be all right when we get home.'

I'm taking it for granted that Dad will make it back to switch off the electricity. Or else home is the last place Stevie will want to be. Home will drive him crazy.

'Stevie.' I'm begging him now. 'Come on, Stevie. Come with me. Don't go with those iron heads.'

'No,' he roars with his blue mouth open wide. 'You leave me alone, you cow. You're just jealous, you are, Rach. You're just trying to get me away from my friends.'

Me jealous of Stevie? What's he talking about?

'What? What did you say?' I ask him in my most dangerous voice, even though I heard him the first time.

He goes frantic—he tries to karate chop my arm so I let go of him. He's quite strong, much stronger than you think.

I let go. 'Ow, that hurt, Stevie. What do you think you're doing?'

I'm still shocked at what he said, about me being jealous. What me, jealous of someone who can't tie his shoe-laces, who can't tell the time? That makes me really mad.

'Go to hell then!' I yell back at him. 'Go with your freaky friends. See if I care. Go on, get lost!'

I'm shaking with rage but at the same time I'm thinking, Oh no, how did this happen?

I've really messed this up. I was supposed to bring Stevie back home. Get him away from the compass-heads. But here we are, on this spooky yellow plain, fighting with each other. Some of the compass-heads notice us yelling. They turn round to stare. Then they go stumbling off again. There's nothing intelligent left in their eyes. Only pain and fear.

'Stevie!'

But he's not going to come with me. And I'm not going to beg him any more. I know Dad said to bring him back but one part of me thinks, Why should I? If he wants to be with them, let him go. I'm not his keeper, am I?

So I do that. I just let him go. Probably couldn't stop him anyway. I can see from his eyes that I've lost him. They're not looking at me any more. They're lifted towards the dunes. Fixed on Alban's fiery torch. He starts walking towards it like he's robot-controlled.

'Stevie.'

I have one last try, even though I know it's hopeless.

'Do you know where they're going? They're going to burn our house down. Like they did the last warden's. Like they did the lighthouse.'

But he doesn't even turn round. He just keeps walking away.

You can see Alban's torch bobbing about in the dunes. It keeps stopping and starting. It's not going very fast. But it's leading the compass-heads towards our house. And now my brother Stevie is with them.

'Alban, why're you doing this?'

But I don't even shout it out, I just mutter it to myself. Even if he could hear me it wouldn't make any difference. He can't help what he's doing. When they get sick they're not in their right minds. That's what Mistress Lodesman said. I'll just have to keep on telling myself that.

Mistress Lodesman. I've just remembered the gates and Mistress Lodesman. It's what we came here for—to bar the gates.

I'm just looking frantically round for her when this voice comes from somewhere: 'Rachel, I can't do this alone.'

She's struggling behind one of the gates, trying to shut it with her shoulder. They're massive wooden gates, like the gates of a castle. I can't help taking one last look at the torch—it's just a red glow in the distance. Then I dash over to help her.

I've always wanted to see inside where the islanders live. But now I've got the chance, it's the last thing on my mind. I catch sight of some green and white—white cottages, green grass. Nothing weird. Except all the houses are facing north. But there's no time to see anything else. Because while we're heaving the gate shut, some islanders are coming out of their houses. They're roaming around looking sick and desperate. But soon they'll lock on to where the pain comes from. And then they'll follow Alban and the others through the dunes to try and stop it.

We've got one of the gates shut.

'The bar, Rachel, we need the bar. It's just inside the gates.'

There's a long plank of wood, lying in the grass against the wall. It's so heavy I think my back's going to crack when I try to lift it.

'I . . . can't . . . shift it.'

But Mistress Lodesman dashes to help and somehow we drag it along.

There are lots of eyes watching us—it makes my skin crawl. I feel better when we're outside the gates again. We leave the bar propped up against the wall while we shove at the other gate with our shoulders.

Just as it's closing I spy through the last little gap.

'They're coming this way.'

'Quick,' says Mistress Lodesman. 'Bar the gates. Quick.'

That's easy to say. There are these iron hook things going across both gates where the bar slots in. But getting it up there nearly kills us. We have to rest the bar on our shoulders and it feels like it's crushing me into the ground but it has to go even higher than that. So we hoist it up like a weightlifter lifts weights and my arms are shaking and I think it's going to come crashing down on my skull when Mistress Lodesman says, 'It's there. Let go.'

And we let the bar drop into place just as someone starts pushing at the inside of the gates.

Then they start tap-tap-tapping like they want to get

out. *Tap tap, tap tap*. It's a really creepy sound. But they can't get out. The gates are barred and the walls are high, like the walls of a fortress.

I look up and up, to the top of the walls. There are flowers growing between the stones. Little pink flowers.

'Couldn't they climb those walls?' I ask Mistress Lodesman.

She doesn't answer.

So I look at her: 'Mistress Lodesman?' and just as I'm looking her face screws up as if she's in pain and she slides down the wall and sort of flops over, like a rag doll, at the bottom of it.

'Mistress Lodesman!'

All sorts of panicky things rush through my head. Maybe she's a compass-head after all—her lips are turning blue. Then she lifts her head and says, gasping between the words. 'Just a little twinge in my heart, Rachel . . . lifting that bar. It'll pass.'

Whump, whump. They're pounding on the inside of the gates. The gates open a crack in the middle. But the bar doesn't give.

'Go and help your father,' says Mistress Lodesman. 'Something is wrong. The electricity . . . it is still on.'

She looks awful—grey and ill. But her green seawater eyes stare into mine.

'Go on, child!' she says, shooing me away with her sternest teacher-voice.

'No, I'm staying.' I sound as wild and confused and scared as the compass-heads.

'Go!' she says in an odd choky voice. 'Find your father.'

And even though she's a sick old woman huddled up against a wall, she can still make you do what she says. Her plait has come loose and her blue waterfall hair is all tangled round her shoulders.

129

'Will you be all right?'

She nods her head. But she won't let me see her face.

'I'll come back for you. Sure you'll be all right?'

She doesn't reply.

I deliberately don't look back. I just turn around and start running, across the plain towards the dunes.

She'll be all right. That's what I'm telling myself. She's a tough old Go-Between. She'll be all right once she's had a rest.

'Concentrate, Rachel.'

I have to tell myself that in my fiercest voice so I don't keep thinking about her. I've got to do what she told me and find my dad.

So I start fighting my way through the dunes.

It's like everything's out to get me. A skyberry bush trips me. Then a spiky gorse rips me. Even the big, white trumpet flowers go *whack* in my face. Then a rabbit burrow grabs my foot and brings me crashing down.

I'm knocked breathless for a minute. It's so warm here in this scoop of sand. It'd be so easy to lie curled up with that sweet coconut smell all round me and close my eyes and just drift away to sleep . . .

'Get up, Rachel, you coward, you total wimp!'

That's me, telling myself off. If anyone else talked to me like that I'd bite their heads off.

So I stagger to my feet and carry on.

Every second I expect to see Alban and the others coming back. I expect to see them plodding back over the top of the next dune. Alban will smile and say, 'Hello, Rachel! What are you doing out here?' And their eyes won't be sick any more and they'll all be peaceful fisherfolk again because Dad's switched the electricity off.

But no one comes over the next dune. There's no one in these dunes but me.

Then I see someone. I almost trip over him. He's kneeling right in front of me, rocking backwards and forwards and moaning.

I don't stop to help him. No fear. It's one of them—the compass-heads. I don't know his name but he was in the gang that followed Alban.

I take a big detour round him and leave him there.

There's another one of them collapsed half-way up a dune. Not dead or anything. Just too ill and weak to follow the others. I don't help her either. I just think, Two down. They're dropping like flies. Can't be many of them left to set fire to our house. Good.

At the top of the next dune I should be able to see our house . . .

There's another one—another collapsed compass-head. This time I hardly notice—I'm getting used to them littering up the dunes. This one's sprawled out in the skyberry bushes. I'm about to hurry by when something catches my eye—a splash of orange. It's Alban. He's hugging his head like it's going to explode. Then he starts beating it into the sand so it leaves a head-shaped hole.

'Help me,' he says.

I crouch down beside him. I've got to be tough—he's a compass-head like the rest of them. He was going to torch our house. So I shake his arm and yell into his ear. 'Where are the others? Where's the torch? Who's got the torch?'

It's useless. He's rolling around and moaning. I don't even think he knows who I am.

So it's stupid to say, 'Alban, I don't know what to do,' because he's not going to help me, is he? But I feel so scared and alone and desperate that I do say it.

Stupid. I should get going, I'm on an urgent mission. So I make myself stand up but the seconds are ticking by and I just stand looking down at him even though I can't bear to see him writhing about, all twisted up and trying to beat his head to bits in the sand.

I take a panicky look around me searching for help. Then I see it—a bright, golden glow like sunrise over the top of the next dune. Only of course I know it's not sunrise. It's our house, all lit up.

'I'll turn the electricity off, Alban. I'll go and do it right now. You'll be all right then, honest.'

I reach down to touch his arm, trying to comfort him somehow. But his arm's thrashing about and it flings me away.

'I have to go now, Alban.'

But he's too far gone to hear me.

As I'm tramping up the next dune a nightmare thought opens out in my mind like an evil flower. 'Maybe it isn't the electricity that's lighting up the sky. Maybe it's a fire. Maybe our house is already on fire . . . '

A hand reaches out from the skyberry bushes and closes round my ankle.

'Get off! Get off!' Something snaps inside my head and I just go berserk, trying to stamp the hand to death like it's a snake.

A long body drags itself from under the bushes. It's got a camouflage jacket on.

'Rachel, Rachel, it's me. Rach!'

It's Dad.

I can feel the breath hissing out of my body like a balloon going down. It's only Dad.

'Dad.' I drop to my knees in the blue bunny poo. 'What you doing under there? Are you a compass-head too?'

I keep seeing them everywhere. I think I'm getting paranoid.

'No, you know I'm not. It's my ankle, Rach. I think I've

broken my ankle. I trapped my foot in one of these damn rabbit holes.'

The skyberry bushes are all smashed down where he's been trying to crawl.

'Oh, Dad . . . ' I'm nearly crying now. I just can't help it. 'What are we going to do?'

Dad grabs my arm. 'Look, Rach. I'll be all right. Go and switch the electricity off. Find your mum!'

I sniff up my tears—two big sniffs.

'There's a switch in the kitchen by the fuse box. Hurry up! Wait a minute,' Dad says. 'Take this with you.' He fumbles around in his pocket. 'Here, Rach.'

It's the electro-magnet.

'Use it,' says Dad. 'If any of them come near you switch it on. Right. Give 'em a few short bursts, on, off, on off, like this.'

'OK, Dad.' But when I take the electro-magnet off him my hand is trembling so much that I almost drop it.

'Go on then!'

I go wading through skyberry bushes to the top of the dune.

And there it is, our house, blazing with electricity, lighting up the dark dunes all around. The windmill is in the back yard. I can't see it from here—but I know it's spinning in the wind.

Stevie's down there, in front of the house. He's got the torch. He's holding it like a weapon. Like he's threatening the house with it—jabbing it at the windows, leaping around like a blue-painted warrior doing a war dance.

The torch is nearly out. But it's still dangerous. There's still crimson glowing at the end of it.

Our front door is wide open. Where's Mum? Stevie stumbles towards the door. There are some others with him. Just a few compass-heads who haven't collapsed in the dunes. Red Fish is there. But he's staggering about like he's drunk. Then *whump* he crashes out onto the sand. And there's only Stevie and me left on our feet.

I go helter-skeltering down the dune.

'Stevie!'

I've got to get past him and into the kitchen to flick that switch to *Off*. He's lurching about but he still tries to block my way.

'Let me through, Stevie!'

I try to push him aside but he's built like a little tank. He just sways a bit then he stabs the torch at me as if to keep me off.

'Ow, Stevie! That hurt!'

There's a red burn-mark on my arm. I have to lick it to stop it stinging.

Right. He's asked for it now.

He turns around, runs his blue tongue over his blue lips and lifts up the torch.

'No! Mum's in there!'

He's going to throw it. Throw it into the hallway and set the house alight. 'No, you don't!'

I zap him with the electro-magnet. Right near his head, rapid pulses like Dad said. One two, one two, one two, one two. It works like a dream. He just crumples into a heap outside the front door. And the torch rolls away into the sand. I jump up and down on it a few times to make sure that it's out. Then I go back to Stevie and bend over him.

For one terrible, heart-stopping second I think I've killed him.

Then he groans and opens his eyes.

'Stevie, I'm sorry. I had to do that. You weren't in your right mind. I had to stop you.'

I've been brought up never, ever to hurt Stevie. Never to upset him even. He's Special Needs and it's not his fault. But when I did it just now, you know, zapped him with the electro-magnet, I felt a little sneaky thrill inside me. Like I was almost enjoying it. But that couldn't be right, could it? That's terrible. Because I love Stevie, I really do. I'd never let anyone hurt him . . .

No time to think about that now. I'll think about it later. I've got urgent things to do.

When I run into the house, it seems like I can *feel* electricity all around me. Buzzing through wires, practically making sparks in the air. It's weird, everything's on, like the house is running itself. The fridge is humming, the washing machine is whirring.

There are voices! 'Mum?' I go racing through to the living room. But it's only the telly in the corner, chattering away to itself.

I go back to the kitchen and do what I should have done straightaway. Click, the house dies all around me. It goes dark and very, very still.

'Mum?'

My voice echoes in the kitchen. Nobody answers. I'm shivering, I feel very cold all of a sudden.

Then I see that the back door is open. It's like history repeating itself. Seems to do that a lot, on Pilot Island.

Mum's run out, hasn't she? She saw them swarming over the dunes like wild men and women instead of the peaceful fisher-folk they're supposed to be. So she got scared and ran. Just like the last warden.

It's getting dark. I should wait for someone who can home. But who knows how long the compass-heads take to recover? It might take them ages. I can't wait that long. I have to find Mum.

So I go racing down to the beach and I'm in the middle of yelling 'Mum!' when a thick white cloud almost swallows me up. Fog. I forgot about the fog. The estuary's full of it, like a great big bowl of fog soup.

Maybe Mum isn't out there. She could be anywhere on Pilot Island. She could be in the house, hiding under the beds. Maybe I'll go back and check under the beds. And in the wardrobes.

But it won't budge out of my brain—that history's repeating itself. That she's out in the estuary somewhere. The more I think about it, the more obvious it seems. As if it's the *only* place she could be. That's what Pilot Island does to your mind. And I'm not even a compass-head.

She's gentle, my mum. Not tough like me. She'll be so scared . . .

And suddenly, big surprise, I feel really calm. I can't home or anything. But Mistress Lodesman can't home and she came out to get me. Wonder if she's OK. Wonder if Alban's getting his right mind back. Wonder if Dad's . . .

'Concentrate, Rach!'

I can't worry about all that now. I've got to find Mum. And like I said before I'm really calm about it. I don't feel afraid any more.

So I just step into the fog like I'm taking a morning stroll. And let it close over my head.

14

Inside the fog that hush comes down. It feels like you're cut off from the world. But it's not a sleepy hush. It's a sort of *waiting* hush, like any second something might jump out at me. Every nerve in my body is on red alert. I'm looking out for signs.

Dry sand, crunchy shells, brown seaweed, wet sand, more brown seaweed, sloppy mud, red seaweed. I'm going further out into the estuary. No good looking out for sea lettuce or trying to smell coconut. They mean safety and I've left that far behind.

Whump, one of the poles across the estuary almost smacks me in the mouth. I hang on to it, hugging it. The top of it is lost in the fog. But I've got a sign. I know where I am. I'm where the water is shallowest. And the tide has turned. It's going out. I can feel it sucking at my shoes.

'Mum!'

No answer.

I'm ankle deep in the sea and hanging on to the pole. Everywhere I turn there's a white wall. Like I'm inside a white envelope.

I can't stay here.

So I fill my lungs full of air and holler loud as I can: 'MUM!'

A tiny voice comes floating back to me: *'Raaaachelllll!'*

She's out there in the estuary. I knew she was. But fog plays tricks with sound. I don't know if she's very near or very far away. She could be so near I could stretch out my hand and touch her.

'Mum, I'm here!'

The pole is all slithery-green. But I'm hanging on as if it's a life belt. Which it is really because if I let go I'll be drifting in the fog like in a white river. I might never find dry land again.

There's another pole out there somewhere—the next pole in line with this one. If I could only reach it. Look for signs.

But it's not as easy as Mistress Lodesman made it look. I wish I could home. Just for, say, half an hour.

'Rach, can you hear me?'

Mum's voice comes wobbling through the fog.

'Rachel, is that you?'

And this time it seems to come from somewhere high up. It's thin and ghostly. This fog must be full of ghosts. All the drowned people whispering and gliding around in it—Asa Lodesman, the engineer, the last warden. The children from the *Mary Ellen* . . .

I think I can hear their little piping voices.

'Stop it, Rachel. It's just some seabirds, that's all. Stop scaring yourself to death! Pull yourself together!'

That's me, of course, giving myself a good telling off. Because I'm scared that, if I don't, I just might fall to pieces.

I'm still clinging on to the pole. In the fog it's like another world. But my head is buzzing with what I've left behind. Mistress Lodesman with her bad heart, Alban trying to beat out his brains. Dad with his busted ankle and Stevie, after I zapped him. It's like a major accident back there—casualties all over the place.

'Rach, I'm in the refuge!'

Mum's voice drives everything else out of my head. I forget about what's happening back on Pilot Island. What's she mean, the refuge? And then I remember.

That's the proper name for the tree-house on stilts. Mum's safe from the fog and the sea and the darkness. She's climbed up the iron ladder into the refuge.

I feel like cheering, 'Yayyy!' But instead I call out, 'I'll come and get you, Mum.'

But I haven't let go of the pole yet. I try to picture it in my head. The refuge is somewhere in the middle of the estuary. But I don't know which direction that is. The fog makes me blind.

Look for signs.

It's impossible. I'm not an Indian tracker.

But then some feathery red seaweed comes floating past me. The seaweed is going out with the tide.

That means the open sea is behind me. Pilot Island is in front of me and if I walk in *that* direction, if I walk dead straight, *across* the current, then I should hit the next pole.

Theoretically, that's what Dad would say. *Theoretically*, Rach.

But I let go of my pole. It's hard to let go, like my hands are Superglued to it. But I force myself and in a second it's swallowed up in the fog. I wade through the waves, small steps, and as long as the red seaweed is washing past me and the water stays shallow I know I'm all right. Mistress Lodesman would be proud of me. Wonder if she's OK?

'Concentrate, Rach.'

Blam, I hit another pole. It nearly breaks my nose but I don't care. I cuddle it like it's my best boyfriend.

'Mum, I'm coming out to get you!'

Just to hear myself say that makes me feel really strong. And I splash off again, without a backward glance this time. It seems like I'm walking for ever. Careful, careful, Rach. Keep to the poles. Watch the way the tide's flowing. Watch for signs. Then I hit a pole that goes clang. It's not a pole at all. It's one of the iron legs of the refuge. And there's the rusty iron ladder disappearing up into the fog.

'Mum!'

'I'm up here!'

I start hauling myself up the ladder.

It's a long, hard, slippery climb. My trainers feel heavy, like wet sponges. The rungs are slimy and weedy and spiky with barnacles.

'Rachel!'

I look up and there's Mum's white face, peering out of the refuge.

She reaches down and hauls me inside on to the wooden floor.

I crouch there for a minute, trying to work out how I'm feeling.

It's the biggest surprise. I feel happy.

I feel dizzy with happiness. I'm so thrilled that I got here and that Mum's safe and that history hasn't repeated itself and that we're not going to join the ghosts in the fog.

It seems like Pilot Island is smiling on us for once.

'Rachel, are you all right?'

'I'm fine.'

Then I get up off the floor to look out the refuge windows. There's no glass in them and no door in the doorway. And it's sort of ramshackle. Just like a tree-house. Except it smells of wet seaweed.

'It's great up here, Mum! It is like a tree-house isn't it? A tree-house at the top of a massive tree. Or at the top of Jack's giant beanstalk. You can see for miles. It's like being on top of the world.'

I can't stop babbling—I'm so relieved. Mum's looking at me with a really weird expression like she's scared I'm cracking up or something.

But it is great up here. It's beautiful. We're in the sky. We're above the fog, in a clear dark-blue sky. And just below us the fog is rolling for miles in every direction. It looks like you could walk out the refuge door straight on to it. Run across it like it's a massive snowy field. But it's not exactly like snow because it's moving all the time— rippling and swirling like the sea does. It's pink at the edges where the sun has just gone down. And there's a pale silver moon over there and the sky is filling up with stars.

'Look, Mum. We're up in the stars!'

Mum rests her hand on my arm. She's got this concerned, bewildered look on her face. She says, 'Rachel, are you sure you're all right?' As if I'm as out of control as the compass-heads.

I take my eyes off the stars and look at Mum. Her face and hair are crusty with salt and mud. She must have fallen over when she ran away. And she's shivering. She's only got a thin shirt on. She's hugging herself with her arms.

'What's going on, Rachel? Where's your dad? Where's Stevie? I tried to find you but I got lost. I saw some islanders coming over the dunes. I couldn't believe it, Rachel. Their eyes, you should have seen their eyes . . . '

And she shakes her head as if she can't find the words to tell me.

'I know, Mum. I know.'

I sit closer to her and put my arms round her to try and stop her shivering. Thought I'd given up protecting people when Stevie said he didn't need me any more. But it's a hard habit to break.

'What's happening, Rach?' Mum says again. 'I just don't understand.'

So I tell her all about the compass-heads. And I have to tell her that Stevie's a compass-head too.

'I can't take all this in,' Mum says, pressing her muddy hands against her head. 'Is all this really true, Rachel?'

'But it'll be all right now,' I tell her, trying to cheer her up. 'Now that the electricity is off. They won't be sick any more. Stevie won't be sick any more.'

'Course, I've missed some bits out of my story. I deliberately haven't told her about Mistress Lodesman's bad heart and Dad busting his ankle in a rabbit hole.

I especially haven't told her that I had to zap Stevie with the electro-magnet. Mum wouldn't understand about that. She'd be really, really upset about it.

There's no point in upsetting her any more. Not when we're stuck out here in a tree-house in the middle of the estuary. I don't like the look of that fog down there. It's getting thicker. It's curling its way up towards us like some horrible creeping plant.

'We have to get back to the island,' says Mum. And she actually puts a foot on the ladder.

'No, Mum. We have to stay up here, until the fog clears.'

'Rachel, we'll die of exposure up here. And anyway, I have to get back to look after Stevie.'

I don't like to tell her that if Stevie needs looking after he'll go to the islanders, not to her. But she might be right about dying of exposure. We're both wet and cold right through to our bones.

The trouble is that I don't fancy risking it twice— finding my way back along the poles to the beach. I got away with it once. I don't know if Pilot Island gives you two chances.

'We have to go back,' Mum keeps saying in this stubborn voice. 'I want to see your dad. I want to see Stevie. All these things you're telling me—I've got to talk about it with your dad.'

An even more worried look comes into her eyes. 'How long did your dad know about all this? Why didn't he tell me?'

'He hasn't known about it long, Mum. Just since today really.'

'I don't understand.' Mum shakes her head hopelessly and her voice gets even more frantic. 'We can't stay here. We have to get back. Come on, Rachel.'

'Mum, it's too dangerous.'

Mum doesn't know about the fog, about how treacherous it is. She spends almost all her time in the schoolhouse. She can't home and she doesn't even know how to look for signs.

We'd be committing suicide. Like Asa Lodesman did. Just thinking about it makes me shiver.

'See,' says Mum, 'your teeth are chattering too. We've no choice. We have to go back.'

The first wispy bits of fog come curling like smoke into the refuge.

Can't Mum see it? Normally, she's a really sensible person. She makes you brush your teeth and eat your greens. But now she's acting really reckless. I don't like her reckless. I like her safe and sensible.

'Everything will be all right back there, Mum. Now the electricity's switched off. Everything will be back to normal.'

'How can you say that, Rachel? When these people tried to burn our house?' (That's another thing I missed out— that it was Stevie who had the torch.) 'When you're saying Stevie's got particles of iron in his brain?'

And she's getting herself into a real state when I hear something. I can't tell if they're near or a long way away—but I hear voices.

'Shhh,' I say to Mum. 'Someone's out there, in the fog.'

It must be them—the compass-heads. Only they would come out here in the darkness and the fog.

I get the electro-magnet out of my pocket. I don't know why I do that. Because there's no need for it is there? The compass-heads have changed back into peace-loving fisher-folk who wouldn't hurt a fly. Haven't they?

'Shhh,' I say to Mum again. But she's already yelling out, 'We're here! We're here!' And she starts climbing down the ladder *clang, clang, clang*. And I'm left alone in the refuge.

Then this joyful voice comes back up the ladder. 'Rach, it's all right. It's Stevie. It's Stevie and Alban. They've come to rescue us.'

I put the electro-magnet away while I'm climbing down. But it's in my hand again when I step off the bottom rung. Just in case.

Then I see Stevie and Alban. Both of them look washed-out and weak. But I can see from their eyes that they're in their right minds.

'Hello, Rach,' says Alban awkwardly.

'Bunch of . . . ,' says Stevie. He doesn't even have to say the words. He just makes his fist into flowers.

Secretly, I slip the electro-magnet back into my pocket.

'How's my dad?' I ask Alban.

'He is fine,' says Alban. 'His ankle was not broken.'

Mum breaks off from firing questions at Stevie. 'Dad's ankle broken! You didn't tell me about that, Rachel.'

'It's *not* broken, Mum.'

'Stay close,' says Alban, as we set off through the fog. 'We will lead you back to Pilot Island.'

His voice sounds grim. His face looks even grimmer. But that's probably because he still feels ill. And, if he remembers what he did when he was ill—such as leading a crazy mob to burn our house down—he's probably a bit embarrassed. I would be if I was him.

'Is Mistress Lodesman OK?' I ask him. 'She's really tough, right? You ought to have seen us lifting that bar! Wow, like Superwoman!'

I bend my arm and make my muscles bulge to show how strong we were. I know I'm acting like a prat. But I'm really happy to see him. And I want him to know it doesn't matter to me what he did. We're still friends.

I'm still grinning when Alban turns round in the fog.

Why isn't he grinning back? Why does he look so tragic?

Then I find out why.

'Rachel, Mistress Lodesman is dead,' he says. 'When we went back we found her outside the gates. And she had died.'

'Died?'

I can't seem to understand what he's telling me. Inside my head there's just sick horror. But the muscles in my face keep on grinning like they did before. I can't seem to stop them. And my mouth is saying stupid things like, 'Are you joking? You mean, she really *died*?'

Alban nods. 'Her heart,' is all he manages to say.

He's not joking. She really died.

And I thought Pilot Island was smiling on us. I must have been as crazy as a compass-head.

Epilogue

Me and Alban are in the middle of the estuary. We're up in the refuge. It's high tide—the sea is sloshing round the iron legs. So we're stuck here until the tide goes down. But we don't mind. We planned it that way.

It's September 4th but it's still warm. Like Dad said, the sky is full of wings. The migrating birds have flown in and they're stuffing themselves with skyberries before they leave to fly south for the winter. I'm leaving myself tomorrow. I'm going back to school on the mainland.

'She's beautiful,' Alban says, his eyes fixed on the horizon.

Some other people are leaving Pilot Island. They're in Asa Lodesman's pilot boat, the *Dove*. She's in full sail and we're watching her from the refuge. She's out in the estuary—heading away from Pilot Island towards the open sea.

'I wish Mistress Lodesman could see her,' says Alban.

And he looks over to Wreckers' Point, as if he can see Mistress Lodesman with her blue waterfall hair standing by the lighthouse. Looking over the estuary with her great-great-grandad's telescope.

Now I know why Asa Lodesman called her the *Dove*. I thought it was a stupid name before. When she was black and hauled up on the beach she didn't look anything like a dove. But she does now, with those white sails lifting her over the water like wings.

Alban waves. Then lets his arm drop. 'They're too far away to see me,' he says.

There are ten islanders aboard her. And she's loaded

146

with skyberry supplies—wine, juice, necklaces. Skyberry bushes to plant when they find somewhere else to live.

'Will they ever come back?' I ask Alban.

'I don't think so,' says Alban. 'I don't think we'll ever see them again.'

'Are you sad?'

He's losing the *Dove* that he worked so hard on. And his uncle and aunt and two of his cousins are sailing away in her. It makes me really sad, to think of them wandering the world—a load of compass-heads in an old sailing boat. Who's going to be their friends?

Alban sighs. 'Nothing could ever be the same could it?' he says. 'Not after we found out about the skyberries. Things had got to change.'

My dad hasn't told anyone on the mainland about the islanders being compass-heads. The islanders don't want him to. 'They don't want to be a freak show,' said Dad, 'with scientists doing blood tests and brain scans and all sorts of experiments on them.'

And anyhow, soon there won't be anyone for the scientists to experiment on. Because there won't be any compass-heads left on Pilot Island. (Except the rabbits.) It was Dad who told the islanders. The iron minerals in your brain are soluble, he told them. So if you stop eating skyberries the minerals will gradually dissolve away. Then you won't have a sixth sense. You'll be just the same as everyone else. But you won't get sick from electricity either. You can go to the mainland. You can even have your own generator. You've got the choice, he told them.

I know what I'd choose if I was a compass-head. Easy peasy. I'd choose to go to the mainland. To have a television and a video and a CD and a computer in my bedroom. I'd never eat another skyberry again.

147

But they didn't think it was easy. It caused terrible arguments. It split families up.

Dad said, 'Sometimes I wish I'd never found out about those bloody skyberries! It's tearing this island apart!'

Things have settled down a bit now. Most islanders stopped eating skyberries and they're already forgetting how to home. A few are leaving to live on the mainland but most are staying. The ones who are staying are talking about getting their own generators.

But some didn't want to change. So they're leaving Pilot Island in the *Dove* to find a new place where compass-heads can live. Hope they find one. What if they don't? Will they wander the world in the *Dove* for ever?

It makes me feel really sad just thinking about it.

But the view from up here is great. The waves are dancing like silver dolphins. And you feel like you're on top of the world. And I'm with Alban. We're here together in our private place where no one can see us. So I can't stay sad for long.

'I was just thinking,' I tell Alban, 'that no one can see us out here. It's a good job Mistress Lodesman's not on Wreckers' Point with her telescope!'

Alban grins. 'She saw everything with that telescope.'

It might sound funny being so cheery when we talk about Mistress Lodesman. But, for days, Alban couldn't talk about her at all. He really missed her and so did I but not as much as him. They've buried her where they bury all the islanders, in a little graveyard inside the walls. And someone carved on her gravestone, 'The Last Go-Between'.

My mum said a really good thing to Alban, when she saw how he was grieving. She said, 'I won't let any of the island children forget her. I'll teach them about her in school. I'll tell them stories about her. How brave she was, what a wise person she was, all the things she did for the island. And I'll tell them about Asa Lodesman too. How he was wrongly accused. How he was the best pilot that ever lived. I'll show them his uniform and his photo. I'll make sure they know the truth.'

'She'd like that,' said Alban. 'She'd really like that.' And afterwards he was a little bit happier.

'Where's Stevie today?' Alban asks me.

He's probably not all that interested. He's probably only asking to take his mind off the *Dove*.

'He's gone to Lincoln with Mum and Dad to buy some new shoes.'

'Has he stopped getting sick?'

'Yes, he can even go under the pylons.'

'Electricity still makes me dizzy,' says Alban. 'It still gives me headaches.'

'Well, that'll stop, won't it? It just takes time. Long as you keep off the skyberries.'

'Why didn't you go with them to the mainland?'

'Didn't feel like it. Rather stay here. They'll probably come back in a bad mood. Stevie's no good in shops. He'll knock something over or throw a wobbly or something.'

'I've never seen Stevie throw a wobbly.'

'Yeah well, he doesn't do it much these days.'

The last one he threw was when Mum told him to stop eating skyberries. She said, 'Those things are poison! They can actually affect your brain! You must promise me never, ever to eat skyberries again!'

And Stevie went berserk and said, 'I won't promise. I won't stop eating them,' and banged his head off the wall like he used to do on the mainland. He said, 'I like being able to home. I like knowing where I am.'

But Red Fish stopped eating them and all his other friends did because they wanted to visit the mainland.

And in the end Stevie did too because he wanted to go to the mainland with them. And I thought he'd hate it when he stopped being able to home. So I taught him to read the signs like Mistress Lodesman taught me.

And you know, he's brilliant at it. Miles better than me. Mistress Lodesman would have been proud. It doesn't matter being clumsy because he can listen and look and smell and remember where things are. Stevie's always been really good at remembering. You have to be when you can't write things down.

So he remembered all the signs—the seaweed and the tidal currents and the sounds you can hear through the fog and what you can smell. And it doesn't matter so much that he can't home any more. He still knows where he is. He feels safe. Even in the dark and the fog and the jungliest dunes.

Stevie's happy. So I don't have to tippy-toe around not upsetting him. I can call him an irritating little brat if I want to.

And, by the way, his bedroom is like World War Three again.

There are a load of fishing boats out on the estuary. They're saying goodbye to the *Dove*. Sailing with her as far as the open sea.

'That's my dad's fishing boat,' Alban says.

'How can you tell? They all look the same to me.'

' 'Course they don't. That's Dad's boat.'

I've met Alban's dad. I've been inside the walls and met all his family. His dad is really tall. He has to duck when he goes through doors. And he wears big clumpy sea boots. He didn't say much at first, he's really shy. But now he says, 'And how are you, Rachel?' whenever he sees me.

'Didn't you want to go with your dad in his boat? To say goodbye to the *Dove*?'

'No,' says Alban, 'I'd rather be up here. I can see her best from up here.'

There's a long silence while we watch the *Dove* sailing down the estuary with all the little boats bobbing around her.

You can see the whole of Pilot Island from up here and a bit of the mainland too. We're like the King and Queen of the Castle.

'Are you going to the mainland tomorrow then?' asks Alban. He sounds casual but he's biting his lip. His lips are pink now like mine, not skyberry blue.

'Yep. But I'm only going to school.'

A seagull flies past the window. *Squawk!* It's surprised to see two people sitting up in the sky.

Alban gives a big sigh and stares at Wreckers' Point again. And I know he's grieving for Mistress Lodesman and his cousins sailing off in the *Dove* and for the way things used to be.

I pat him on the shoulder, try to cheer him up. 'You always wanted to go to the mainland, didn't you? You said so. And now you can, whenever you like!'

'I know. But now I can go whenever I like, it doesn't seem so important any more.'

'But it's much better not getting sick, isn't it? I mean, it was really scary when you all got sick. Falling down and throwing up, *yuuurgh!* and everything. And you don't have to shut yourselves inside those walls any more—you could even take them down if you wanted to . . . '

It's windy up here and Alban's long, black hair is blowing over his face. When he pushes it out of the way I can see he's grinning a shaky grin at me. Good, he's cheering up.

'Yes,' he says. 'It's much better not getting sick. I forgot how awful that was.'

The *Dove* is sailing towards the horizon. You can see her white sails sliding across the blue sky. The little fishing boats around her are just dots.

There's something I want to ask Alban. But it makes me feel nervous just thinking about it. Like lots of tiny wings are beating inside me.

But I've got to ask him. So I take a couple of deep breaths. 'So . . . what are you going to do, then?'

'What about?'

'Are you staying on Pilot Island? 'Cos *we're* staying, me and Stevie and Dad and Mum.'

'I thought you were going away.'

'Yeah, but only to school in Lincoln. I told you. I'll be back at night.'

'I thought you were staying with someone called Sophie.'

'Only sometimes, when I have to because of the tides. But most nights I'll be coming back.'

I'm surprised to hear myself saying that. I'm not sure when I changed my mind. When I decided that I'd rather come back to Pilot Island than stay with Sophie.

I'm even more surprised when Alban says, 'I might come to Lincoln myself. There's a college there. I might go to it.'

My stomach clenches up like a fist. 'So you are going away, then!'

'Only during the day like you.'

'Oh, yeah, right.' I can breathe again now. I was holding my breath before and I didn't realize it.

'What are you going to learn at this college?'

'How to do what Mistress Lodesman did. We've been talking about it, me and Dad and the others that are left.

They still need someone to do business with the mainland—you know, the oyster farm and the crab and lobster fishing. It's how we live.'

Suddenly I understand what he's saying. A big grin spreads all over my face. 'You're going to be the next Go-Between! Wow, you'll be really important!'

Alban looks embarrassed. 'No,' he says. 'Mistress Lodesman was the last real Go-Between. I could never take her place. Besides, we don't need a Go-Between—any of us can visit the mainland now.'

'You'll still be a *sort of* Go-Between though.'

'Well, not like her.'

But he looks really pleased.

We look out again over the estuary. And we're just in time to see the *Dove* disappear. One second her white sails are there. Then they're gone.

I can't help thinking about the islanders inside her. The ones who wanted to stay compass-heads. I hope they find somewhere where there's no electricity and where they can plant their skyberry bushes. And where they won't have to change. Is there a place like that in the world?

The little fishing boats aren't going any further with the *Dove*. They're letting her go. They're turning round now and coming back to Pilot Island.